"I see his father is listed as 'unknown.' "

Bryn was studying the certificate Lian had handed him, his expression difficult to define.

Her shrug was defensive. "What else could I say? All I had was a first name. I couldn't even remember your last."

"Until you saw it in the magazine article." The implication of his remark was clear.

"Do you really see me as a con artist?" Cheeks flushing, she forced herself to hold the sardonic gaze.

His gray eyes scanned her delicate features, coming to rest on the soft fullness of her mouth. "Looks can be deceptive. The best confidence tricks are perpetrated by the least questionable."

"That's a cynic's viewpoint."

He made a mock bow. "Guilty as charged."

KAY THORPE, an English author, has always been able to spin a good yarn. In fact, her teachers said she was the best storyteller in the school—particularly with excuses for being late! Kay then explored a few unsatisfactory career paths before giving rein to her imagination and hitting the jackpot with her first romance novel. After a roundabout route, she'd found her niche at last. The author is married with one son.

Books by Kay Thorpe

HARLEQUIN PRESENTS
1141—LAND OF ILLUSION
1204—TOKYO TRYST
1261—SKIN DEEP
1301—STEEL TIGER
1356—AGAINST ALL ODDS
1397—INTIMATE DECEPTION

HARLEQUIN ROMANCE
2151—TIMBER BOSS
2232—THE WILDERNESS TRAIL
2234—FULL CIRCLE

Don't miss any of our special offers. Write to us at the following address for information on our newest releases.

Harlequin Reader Service
P.O. Box 1397, Buffalo, NY 14240
Canadian address: P.O. Box 603,
Fort Erie, Ont. L2A 5X3

KAY THORPE

night of error

Harlequin Books

TORONTO • NEW YORK • LONDON
AMSTERDAM • PARIS • SYDNEY • HAMBURG
STOCKHOLM • ATHENS • TOKYO • MILAN

Harlequin Presents first edition March 1992
ISBN 0-373-11446-X

Original hardcover edition published in 1990
by Mills & Boon Limited

NIGHT OF ERROR

CHAPTER ONE

ETCHED against a lowering sky, the high fells looked dark and forbidding. An omen of what was to come, perhaps, thought Lian, allowing trepidation to gain a temporary hold. Bryn Thornley was certainly dark, and hardly likely to greet what she had to say to him with a sunny smile. That was providing she even got to see him at all.

So her first priority was to make sure of it, she told herself resolutely. If he wasn't at home today, then she would simply have to make the journey again—and keep on making it until she succeeded in her aim. A letter was unlikely to elicit anything but a summary dismissal of her claim. Face to face, he would have to pay attention.

'Where are the lakes, Mummy?' asked the small boy seated at the bus window. 'I don't see any water!'

'I'll take you to Windermere this afternoon,' Lian promised. 'That's the very biggest one.' She lightly touched her son's dark head, resisting the urge to hug him to her in an excess of motherly love. At four and a half, Jonathan was apt to regard such displays as beneath his dignity—in public, at least. 'We'll have lunch in a café first,' she added with a recklessness unsupported by the amount she had left in her purse.

Little chance of being invited to eat at Revedon, came the wry thought. The kind of shock she was planning to inflict was hardly scheduled to turn Bryn Thornley's mind in the direction of food for a while. Opening her handbag, she took out the much-read magazine cutting

for yet another perusal. Not that there was anything left
to glean from the facts presented, but it helped to have
them fresh to mind.

The colour photograph showed a tautly boned, intelligent face, hair thick and crisply styled, skin lightly
tanned and free of blemish but for a small scar just to
the right of the mouth. The latter served to emphasise
the sardonicism in that faintly slanted smile. A man who
saw the world through eyes untainted by anything even
faintly rose-coloured, at a guess.

The article itself was pretty short. Probably because,
Lian reflected, the interviewee had declined to tender very
much personal detail. A prominent industrialist, he had
inherited Revedon Manor on his father's death just two
years ago, reopening it to the public this last Easter after
extensive restoration work. The writer enthused about
both the house and, in a rather different manner, the
man himself. The fact that at thirty-five he was still
unmarried made him even more worthy of note. 'One
of the county's most eligible bachelors up for grabs by
any woman capable of broaching his defence system'
was the final and somewhat cynical comment. It didn't,
Lian acknowledged ruefully, create much confidence in
her own ability to reach him.

He'd been different five years ago; he must have been,
or she wouldn't have been drawn to him in the first place.
But then, she'd altered too. She'd had to alter. Bringing
up a child on one's own called for more than one kind
of sacrifice.

Not that she'd be without Jonathan, of course. He
made everything worthwhile. All the same, she owed it
to him to do what she could to secure him a better future
than she could offer alone.

Carrying estate employees as well as paying visitors from Kendal, the single-decker bus was almost full. A tour guide would no doubt be provided to show each party around the house, which would mean seizing any opportunity which presented itself. Whatever happened, she wasn't leaving Revedon until she had either seen Bryn Thornley in person, or assured herself that he wasn't in residence. If the latter, then she might possibly leave the letter she had written just in case, and hope her instincts were wrong in believing he would simply ignore it. No man could surely turn his back on his own son?

They were turning into the estate now between huge iron gates swung back to allow access to all motorised traffic, slowing for the cattle-grid spanning the gateway. A small herd of red deer grazing at the edge of the belt of woodland flanking the grassy slope paid scant attention to their passing. Jonathan looked at them in wide-eyed wonderment.

'Does Father Christmas live here?' he asked in his carrying treble, drawing wide smiles from those in the immediate vicinity.

'No, but he sometimes comes to borrow a few for his sleigh,' said the young man occupying the seat immediately behind. 'There's a tame one over at the children's enclosure. Rabbits and guinea pigs too.'

Grey eyes took on an incandescent shine. 'Are we going there, Mummy?'

Lian hesitated, torn between wanting to say yes, and the knowledge that no hard and fast plans could be made until she had done what she was here to do. 'It depends how much time we have,' she temporised. 'We'll certainly try to fit it in.'

'You can get a snack at the tea-bar if you're thinking about where to eat,' volunteered the young man. 'Mr Thornley had part of the old stables converted.'

Lian turned to look at him properly for the first time, seeing a freckled, pleasantly featured face and an appealing smile. He was dressed casually in open-necked shirt and lightweight bomber jacket, his fairish hair cut short and curly. She found herself smiling back.

'You're employed at Revedon?'

'A groundsman,' he supplied. 'I'd have been here three hours ago, except that I had to pick some things up for Dad. He's head gardener,' he added with a certain pride. 'Been at Revedon for forty years. There's a lot more of us since Mr Thornley took over. We're just starting to get the grounds back to what they should be.'

Lian kept her tone light. 'He's a good man to work for, then?'

'A fair one,' came the answer. 'Providing you stick at it, that is. Those who don't soon get the push. He doesn't take things too easy himself, so you can't expect him to let others get away with it. The Duchess keeps the household staff on their toes too.'

Lian lifted surprised eyebrows. 'The Duchess?'

He grinned. 'Mrs Thornley. We call her that because she looks like one. My name's Robert, by the way. Robert Waterhouse. You're not from Kendal, are you?'

Lian shook her head. 'Manchester. We came up by coach.'

'Just to see the house?'

'It's not very far,' she responded lightly, 'and there's plenty more to see round and about too. I just happen to be interested in old houses.'

'Along with a whole lot more, if the crowds who've been turning up since we opened again are anything to go by.' He nodded at the window. 'There it is now. Big, isn't it?'

Set against a heavily wooded hillside, the turreted and crenellated building was certainly no mean size. Not exactly beautiful, Lian thought, yet with a lot of character. She counted no less than a dozen chimneys scattered among the gabled roofs. A small ornamental lake lay over to the left, with a fountain spouting several feet into the air, and what looked like a brace of swans over by the far bank. The private gardens lay behind the house, enclosed by tall stone walls.

'Is Mr Thornley here this weekend?' she asked on what she hoped was a casual note.

'Saw him arrive yesterday afternoon,' Robert confirmed. 'You'll be able to take the first tour at half-past ten. There's three guides on weekends. Depends who you get as to how long it lasts. Mrs Baxter's the best value for money. What she doesn't know about Revedon isn't worth knowing.' The grin came again. 'My sister, if you're wondering. She's married to Joe Baxter at Home Farm.'

'The farm is part of the estate too?'

'That's right. Mind you, Joe gets a pretty free hand running it. There have been Baxters at Revedon for more than two hundred years.'

Lian smiled. 'You sound well genned up on things yourself.'

'I should be after listening to Dorothy going on about it all for years.' He was leaning forward in his seat, an elbow propped on the back of hers, eyes roving her small fine features under the mass of chestnut-brown hair in frank appreciation. 'Your husband not like this sort of thing, then?'

It took an effort to keep the smile from stiffening. She had never attempted to pretend she was married, and didn't intend starting now, but neither did she see any reason to tell a complete stranger the story of her life. 'You could say that,' she prevaricated.

The bus was turning into a wide car park off to one side of the house. People were already getting to their feet in readiness for the stop. As if on cue, the sun broke through the cloud cover to warm the old stone pile, drawing a concerted cheer from the visitors.

'Hope you enjoy your visit,' said Robert, after lifting Jonathan down the bus step, much to the latter's disgust. 'Might see you if you decide to have a walk round the grounds after. I'll be working till one.'

Lian made some vague reply. The closer she came to fulfilling her aim, the more she realised how difficult it was going to be. She had been unable to make any definite plan of campaign because she hadn't been sure what circumstances might arise. Once inside the house, she would simply have to play it by ear.

The ticket kiosk was situated just within the wrought-iron gates which in turn led through to an enclosed courtyard. An entrance fee of one pound fifty plus fifty pence for Jonathan depleted her meagre store of cash to a point where lunch might be something of a problem. She could have saved the two pounds by going round to the main door and asking to see Mr Thornley right away, except that some reason would have to be provided, and she wasn't prepared to divulge that to anyone else but the man himself. This was her only other recourse.

Waiting for the group to gather in the small side hall was a youngish, fair-haired woman Lian took to be the famed Mrs Baxter—a guess confirmed by the amount of detail imparted during the first fifteen minutes of the tour. Mind occupied with other matters, she paid only scant attention to the series of beautiful eighteenth-century rooms, although Jonathan was overawed by the sheer magnificence of the place, so different from the tiny flat he called home.

'Do any children live here?' he demanded of the guide at one point, receiving a smiling negative in reply.

'Would you like to live here yourself?' asked the woman, and elicited a decided shake of the small dark head.

Of no consequence, Lian reflected drily. What she wanted from Bryn Thornley didn't include a home; they already had one of those, inferior though it might be.

They were mounting the west half of the grand staircase when she saw the door marked 'Private' at the half-landing. Under the guise of adjusting her shoelace, she allowed the rest of the party to forge on ahead, then tentatively turned the door-handle.

Finding it unlocked, she gave herself no further time to consider her actions, but seized Jonathan's hand and drew him with her through to a short corridor culminating in another flight of stairs. A totally different world in here, the deep blue carpet fitted in modern style and still holding the smell of new wool.

'Where are we going?' asked Jonathan with interest as they mounted the stairs.

A good question, Lian acknowledged. One assumed that a door marked 'Private' would eventually bring them into contact with members of the household proper. As it was unlikely she was going to happen on Bryn Thornley by accident, she had to be prepared to stand her ground when they did run across someone. Short of throwing her out of the place bodily, there was no way they'd get her to leave without seeing the master of the house; on that point she was adamant. Opportunity had to be grasped with both hands. Teeth too, if necessary!

Confrontation came sooner rather than later. Reaching the top of the flight, she stood irresolutely for a moment looking from side to side of the corridor going in both directions. There were several doors in sight. One of them opened to emit a thin, middle-aged woman dressed in plain grey, whose somewhat dour features took on a look of impatience when she saw the two of them standing there.

'Can't you people read?' she demanded. 'The door back there says private! It should be locked, anyway.'

Lian took a steadying breath, refusing to allow the woman to intimidate her. 'It obviously wasn't or I wouldn't be here. I'm looking for Mr Thornley.'

The woman laughed shortly. 'I'm sure you are. What is it, some charity you want a contribution to?'

Close, Lian thought. Aloud she said flatly, 'My business is with Mr Thornley. Would you take me to him, please?'

'I most certainly will not!' The impatience gave way to righteous indignation. 'I don't know who you think you are, young woman, but Mr Thornley doesn't see anyone without an appointment. You'll have to contact the estate controller's office and make one through the proper channels. Now, if you'll kindly turn around and go back the way you came.'

'No.' Lian was aware of Jonathan's widened stare, but nothing was going to stop her now. 'If you won't take me, I'll have to find him for myself.'

In other circumstances the woman's expression might have been almost laughable. She looked so totally at a loss for words. 'I've never heard anything like it,' she spluttered. 'Who do you think you are?'

'You already said that,' Lian pointed out, and then on a softer note, 'Look, all I want is to speak with him. You won't be blamed for anything.'

'No, I won't, because it isn't going to happen.' The other was beginning to recover from disconcertion, her expression firming again. 'If you don't leave immediately, I'll have to call one of the male staff to deal with you!'

Lian firmed her own expression. 'The only way you're going to get me out is by force, and if anyone here lays a hand on me *or* my son I'll charge them with assault!'

The housekeeper, if that was what she was, looked close to apoplexy. 'Don't you dare threaten me!' she shouted. 'I'll be the one to call the police in, you . . . you——!'

A door further down the corridor opened abruptly, the man who emerged gazing at the little group by the stairs in obvious displeasure. 'What the devil's going on, Mrs Banks?' he demanded. 'I'm trying to read a report in here!'

'I'm sorry, sir.' The woman's voice had quietened, her face reflecting discomfiture. 'I was just trying to convince this young lady that she couldn't come and see you without a proper appointment.'

'My name is Downing,' Lian put in swiftly as the man's eyes shifted from the older woman to her. 'Lian Downing. I have to speak to you . . . Bryn.'

Dark brows lifted as he studied her, a curious expression crossing the well-defined features. 'Do I know you?' he asked.

You did once, she thought. Only too well! 'I'd prefer to talk in private,' she said. The smile she gave Mrs Banks was apologetic. 'I'm sorry if I upset you, but I didn't have any choice. I wonder if you'd be kind enough to

look after Jonathan for me while I'm with Mr Thornley?'
She took the agreement for granted, turning a rather
more reassuring smile on her son. 'It won't take too long,
then we can go and look at those animals you wanted
to see.'

Jonathan looked a little uncertain, but he nodded
assent. It was the housekeeper herself who seemed about
to argue, until Bryn Thornley spoke.

'That's all right, Mrs Banks. Why don't you take the
child down to the kitchen and give him some lemonade?'
To Lian he added, 'You'd better come on in.'

She gave her son's small shoulder a brief touch in
passing. Gregarious by nature, he would not be thrown
off his stride for long. If he followed true to form, he
would have made a fan even of the dour Mrs Banks by
the time they were ready to leave.

Bryn Thornley stood aside to allow her prior passage
into the room. He was even taller than she remembered
him, his body lean and muscular in the fine cord trousers
and short-sleeved white shirt. Grey eyes bored into her
as she passed him, tautening every nerve in her body.
The closing of the door in her wake gave her a sense of
being trapped.

The room was lined with bookshelves, the décor
restrained, the furnishings wholly masculine and businesslike. A leather armchair faced a chesterfield placed
at right angles to the huge stone fireplace, the latter at
present lit by a tasteful display of spring flowers. He
invited her to take a seat, perching himself on the arm
of the chair opposite to regard her with a certain
speculation.

'You have me at a disadvantage,' he said. 'Where did
we meet?'

Lian drew in a deep breath. The next few minutes were going to be crucial to Jonathan's future. 'It was over five years ago, and comparatively briefly, so I can't blame you for forgetting.'

'Five years?' The line had deepened between the dark brows. 'You'd have still been in school then, I imagine.'

Green eyes held grey without faltering. 'I was nineteen at the time. We met at a party in Manchester. You were bored so you suggested we left and had dinner together somewhere. Afterwards...' there was just the faintest of tremors in her voice '...we went back to your hotel suite.'

Some unreadable expression flickered briefly across his face. 'And?'

This time the breath she drew was ragged. 'You made love to me. It was my first time. Perhaps you'd remember that much?'

His smile lacked any element of humour. 'Perhaps I would. Virgins are outside my code of ethics—providing I know in advance, that is. You looked very different that night.' He gave her no time to comment. 'If it's compensation you're after, you left it a bit late. My conscience has its own statute of limitations.'

'It isn't,' Lian denied. 'At least, not for me.' When it came right down to it, there was only one way to say it, and that was straight out. 'I got pregnant. Your son was born the following January. You saw him a few minutes ago.'

All expression had been wiped from his face. He looked turned to stone. Recovery was admirably swift considering.

'Am I really expected to take that claim seriously?' he asked with hard derision. 'The child could be anybody's!'

'Except that he isn't,' she returned on as level a note as she could manage. 'Believe it or not, you're the only man I ever...knew that way.'

'Convenient.' His tone cut. 'So how come I wasn't presented with the facts of the matter until now?'

'Because I never knew who you were until I happened to pick up an old copy of the magazine carrying your photograph a couple of weeks ago. You'd been brought to the party by some business acquaintance, you said. I didn't know anyone there well enough myself to start trying to trace you.'

'What about your family?'

Voice wooden, she said, 'My mother wanted me to have the pregnancy terminated.'

'Obviously she failed to convince you.'

Her head came up sharply, eyes acquiring a brilliant emerald glitter. 'I don't subscribe to abortion! And I wouldn't be without Jonathan. I wouldn't be here telling you this at all if it weren't for the fact that he merits something better than I can provide for him on a limited income. He's due to start school proper in January. If I could afford the fees, he'd be going to a good private school, but I can't. The only reason I can top up my single-parent entitlement with a part-time job is because a friend very kindly looks after him for me on the days when he isn't in nursery school. It enables me to provide food and clothing and a roof over our heads, but precious little else. If...' Her voice caught suddenly; she dropped her gaze, knuckles clenching white on the sofa arm. 'It cost me a great deal to come here like this,' she got out. 'I never asked anyone for anything in my life before. Only he is your son, and that means you should be given a chance to share the responsibility.'

The silence after she finished speaking was lengthy. Bryn was the first to move, rising abruptly to his feet to stand with hands thrust into trouser pockets. 'You still have to convince me that he's my son. What proof can you show me?'

Lian pulled herself together to reach for her handbag and extract the long envelope. 'Here's his birth certificate. I'd have had to go more or less straight from you to some other man for the timing to fit so closely. Then there's photographs of him from a baby up until a few months ago. He looks just like you. If you'd given him more than a passing glance in the corridor just now, you might have seen the resemblance for yourself.'

He was studying the certificate she had handed him, his expression difficult to define with any accuracy. 'I see you have the father down as unknown.'

Her shrug was defensive. 'What else could I say? All I had was a first name—I couldn't even remember your last.'

'Until you saw it in the magazine article.'

The imputation was only too clear. Cheeks flushing a little, she forced herself to hold the sardonic gaze. 'I recognised you from the photograph. I'd been looking at your image for four and a half years. Bryn isn't exactly a common name either.' She spread her hands in a gesture of appeal. 'Do you really see me as a con-artist?'

The grey eyes scanned her delicately sculpted features, coming to rest on the soft fullness of her mouth and acquiring a certain ironic recognition. 'Looks can be deceptive. The best confidence tricks are perpetrated by the least questionable.'

'That's a cynic's viewpoint.'

He made a mock bow. 'Guilty as charged. I never found all that much to be optimistic about where people are concerned.'

'Particularly women?' she challenged. 'Your past affairs do seem to have been pretty short-lived.'

The smile he slanted was short on appreciation. 'Journalists tend to leave few stones unturned. My affairs, past, present, or to come, have little bearing on the matter in hand. Supposing you tell me exactly what it is you're after?'

'I thought I already had,' she said. 'I don't want your money for myself. I don't even need to handle it. All I ask is that you set up some kind of arrangement to take care of those needs I can't cover.'

'You seem to have it all worked out,' he commented drily, drawing another defensive shrug.

'It isn't a lot to ask from someone in your position— and Jonathan does have rights, even if he is illegitimate.'

'If I accept him as my son, I'd have certain rights too.' His voice was silky smooth, and dangerous with it. 'Have you considered that?'

'I very much doubt if you'd want to be saddled with a small boy on any permanent basis,' returned Lian with what coolness she could muster. 'In any case, the courts always favour the mother.'

'Even where the father could provide a far better standard of living?' He shook his head at the look on her face, his mouth derisive. 'There's risk attached to every venture. Would you be prepared to pay the price if it came to it?'

It was Lian's turn to shake her head. The suspicion that she might have made a bad mistake was beginning to filter into her mind. 'I'd never let him go!' she denied fiercely. 'And if this is your way of trying to get rid of me, it won't work! I spent too much time nerving myself to come here at all to go back without achieving what I came for.'

'Mightn't a letter have been a better idea initially?' he asked. 'At the very least, it would have reduced the shock.'

She looked back at him with unconcealed scepticism. 'Would you have believed it more readily because it was written down?'

'I might have.'

'I doubt it. In fact, I think you'd have simply binned it.'

There was a brief pause, then broad shoulders lifted. 'You could be right at that. Only don't run away with the idea that I'm totally won over even now. Coincidence doesn't constitute proof.'

'So have Mrs Banks bring Jonathan back up,' Lian challenged. 'You'll not be able to doubt it once you get a good look at him. I could hardly believe it myself when I opened that magazine and saw your face gazing out at me. He even has the same nose. A bit too strong for his face right now, but he'll grow into it.'

'Does he know why you're here?'

'Of course not.'

'Don't you think it's going to be rather a shock for him to be confronted with a father right out of the blue?'

'He doesn't have to know who you are,' Lian returned evenly. 'So far as he's concerned, his daddy went away before he was born. That's as much as he's needed to know up to now. Naturally, I'll tell him the truth when he's old enough.'

'But not his father's name?'

Her lip curled a little. 'No. So you don't need to fear his suddenly turning up as a teenager when you're married with a family of your own. I shall tell him I never knew your full name.'

Grey eyes considered her thoughtfully. 'That's hardly going to show you in a very good light.'

'The price of wrong-doing,' she responded without particular inflexion. 'If he grows into half the man I think he will, he'll make allowances for human weakness.'

'There's nothing weak about his mother,' came the ironic comment. 'I'd say your nerve was second to none!'

If only he knew, Lian reflected wryly. Sitting here, she felt as if she had been put through a wringer; the perspiration was still trickling down her back. For Jonathan, she'd had to keep telling herself. For her son, who hadn't asked to be born and who merited every effort on her part to gain him at least a small part of his birthright. Once the arrangement she wanted had been made, they need neither of them ever see Bryn Thornley again.

'You only mentioned your mother,' he said now. 'What about the rest of your family?'

'My father died when I was fifteen,' she answered expressionlessly. 'I don't have any brothers or sisters, and I haven't seen my mother in five years.'

'You're saying she threw you out because of the baby?'

'Not physically. It was just better for us both that I left.' Lian made a brief gesture. 'She had a certain standing in the community to consider. An illegitimate grandchild wouldn't have helped her image. She's married again since—a financier called Brian Cleeves. You may know of him.'

'Yes.' Bryn's tone was abrupt. 'How did you cope on your own?'

She smiled faintly. 'I joined a commune. I wasn't the only unmarried mother. When Jonathan was six months old I managed to get a council flat and find myself a part-time office job. A neighbour looks after him for me. She has two small children of her own, so another one doesn't make much difference.'

If the tale elicited any sympathy in her listener, it didn't show. 'Hardly the kind of environment you must have grown up in,' he commented.

'The kind of environment I grew up in doesn't produce people as kind and caring as the ones I've met since moving out,' Lian returned. 'I wouldn't go back, even if I were offered the chance.'

'I'm sure.' The scepticism came over loud and clear. 'Assuming just for the moment that I accepted responsibility, what kind of figure would you have in mind as a settlement?'

Meeting his gaze full on, Lian contained her feelings with an effort. 'I already told you, it isn't a lump sum I'm after. What I'd like you to do is set up a kind of trust fund out of which essential expenses could be paid without any money actually coming into my hands at all. I can take care of my own needs quite comfortably.'

'But you'd still be living in a council flat?'

'There's nothing wrong in that,' she countered. 'Plenty of other people do it.'

'And send their children to the local schools.'

'Not always. I have a neighbour who goes out cleaning in order to put her son through private schooling. And before you ask me why I can't do the same,' she tagged on swiftly as he made to speak, 'there's a husband to provide the basics for all of them.'

'Don't jump the gun,' advised Bryn Thornley drily. 'It hadn't occurred to me to suggest any such thing.'

There was a lengthy pause; his eyes were narrowed as if in contemplation. When he spoke again it was with purpose. 'Stay where you are. I'll be back.'

Lian watched him move to the door with the lithe and easy stride that bespoke perfect fitness and health. Fragments of memory kept coming back to taunt her: the deeply tanned, silken sheen of his skin; the power in the arms wrapped about her; the sensual movement of those firm lips against hers, lifting her into realms she had never known existed. Five years ago, yet it could have been yesterday...

CHAPTER TWO

'FANTASTIC!' Phillip had said in the car. The impression she had been aiming for, Lian supposed, studying her image in the powder-room mirror. Cut low enough to reveal the firm swell of her breasts, the red dress certainly made her look older, as did the upswept hairstyle and professionally applied make-up. Useful having a friend training to become a beautician, even if said career wasn't quite what her fond parents had had in mind for her. The eyes alone were a work of art.

The invitation to accompany Phillip to this party had come out of the blue only this morning. Four years older than she was herself, and the pivot of most of her girlhood dreams, he had paid no more than a passing attention to her since he began making his way in the world. Which was why she had to make the most of this opportunity—and it seemed to be working. His eyes had certainly opened wide enough on first sight of her tonight.

And not only Phillip's either, if the attention she was receiving from other male guests was anything to go by. There was a lot to be said for a new approach to the way one looked. It even made a difference to the way one acted.

The party was in full swing when she went out again. Large as it was, the house itself was almost bursting at the seams with people in various stages of merry-making. A twenty-first for the daughter, Phillip had said, although not all the guests were of the younger generation.

Phillip himself was nowhere in sight. He could, Lian supposed, have gone to get them both another drink. She had already had a great deal more than she was accustomed to drink, but, with champagne flowing like water, who was counting?

Some young man she'd never seen before whirled her into a room cleared for dancing, laughingly ignoring her half-hearted protests.

'You're stunning!' he told her. 'Absolutely stunning! Emma was pea-green!'

'Emma?' Lian queried.

'Phil's ex. They had a bust-up a few days ago. Didn't he tell you?'

Obviously not, she wanted to reply, or she wouldn't be asking, but the nasty suspicion already beginning to raise its head kept her quiet. Phillip was using her; all he'd wanted was a partner to bring to the party to arouse this Emma's jealousy.

'I'm assuming she's here tonight?' she asked.

'Sure. In fact, I saw the two of them together only a few minutes ago, kissing and making up.' He added with deliberation, 'Which leaves you free to do your own thing. How about sticking with me?'

The hurt of it made her tart. 'There's no glue that strong!'

'Quick-witted too!' He was grinning, refusing to take umbrage. 'How about I grab us another couple of glasses for starters?'

About to refuse, Lian abruptly changed her mind. She might feel like crawling away to lick her wounds in a dark corner somewhere, but she wasn't going to do it. Phillip mustn't guess how she felt about him—mustn't ever realise what hopes she had entertained about this evening. She was going to stick it out and smile all the way, if it killed her! And it might just do that, too.

There was a measure of comfort to be found in alcohol, she discovered over the following hour or so. It might not cancel out the hurt completely, but it certainly deadened it. She lost count of how many glasses of champagne she consumed. She also lost count of how many different partners she danced with. The urge to show Phillip how little she needed him outweighed all other considerations.

At which point she first became aware of the man leaning against the wall near the door, she couldn't afterwards remember. All she did recall was the tingle that speculative grey regard sent down the length of her spine when she happened to catch it full on. He was one of the older brigade—at least thirty—and conservatively dressed in a pale grey suit. Anyone else standing alone in a crowded room might have looked a little uncomfortable, but not him. He had an air of self-sufficiency Lian suddenly longed to disrupt—if only to prove that she could.

Breaking away from her present partner, who carried on dancing without her in a state of happy inebriation, she floated across to confront the older man with an inviting little sparkle.

'Why don't you come and dance? No one should be alone at a party!'

He came away from the wall without haste, his smile slow and stomach-churning. 'Not when there's someone like you around,' he agreed. 'I've been watching you for the past twenty minutes. Don't you ever get tired?'

'Never!' she laughed. 'Life's too short to waste a single minute of it!'

'A philosophy I can go along with.' He shook his head as she made to draw away from him in order to perform the gyrations called for by the music. 'Not like that.'

Something tautened deep down inside her as he pulled her into his arms. She was fairly tall for a girl herself, but even in her high heels she found her eyes were still only on a level with his mouth. She followed the clean line of his jaw to where the short, dark sideburns began, then up and over crisply styled hair and down again to be seized and mesmerised by the steely impenetrability of the grey eyes. Steely only for a moment before the slow smile warmed them.

'Assessment over?' he asked.

With the music so loud, she was forced to turn an ear towards his mouth in order to hear what he was saying. She felt his lips touch her lobe in a caress that made her blood sing, resisting the impulse to jerk away because the sensation was so pleasurable. His hands at her back were firm and commanding, holding her close enough for her to feel the hard muscularity of his thighs against hers. She had never known such total disruption of composure before. It was like being hit with a truck.

To make herself heard, she slid her arms about his neck to bring her mouth closer to his ear, feeling a tremor run through her at the increased pressure against her breasts from his chest. 'Who are you?'

'The name's Bryn,' he mouthed back. 'And you?'

She told him her first name, no longer sure whether the light-headedness she was feeling was from champagne or being too close to his sheer male magnetism. She wanted to melt in his arms, to have that strong, faintly cruel mouth of his on hers in a kiss she knew would be like nothing she had experienced before. Older men were so sure of themselves—so unlike the boys her own age.

'Are you with anyone in particular?' he asked at her ear, and his breath was a caress in itself.

'No one,' she denied, steeling herself against the sudden shaft of pain. 'No one at all.'

'Then I think we should get out of here,' he said. 'I can't take this racket much longer.'

Lian made no attempt to withdraw the hand he clasped as he started for the door. Getting out of this racket seemed a good idea. Never a better one! She had a vague notion that someone called out her name, but it didn't stop her from following the man whose lean, yet powerful build was forging a pathway through the throng around the door. His hand felt so warm and strong about hers, the fingers long and tensile. Bryn. Only a man of his stature could carry a name like that.

Things ran together a little after that. She was aware of climbing into a vehicle of some kind—probably a taxi—of arriving at some intimately lit restaurant and nibbling her way through a variety of dishes without eating a very great deal, of conversing with vivacity and eloquence on a number of subjects and flirting outrageously with this man who was making her forget the hurt of rejection, if only for an hour or two.

Eventually, there was another taxi to one of the city's top-class hotels, a sojourn in the bar where they were served more drinks, and a ride up in a lift with Bryn at her side and her head in the clouds. This was living with a capital 'L'—the kind of evening she'd only hitherto read about in magazine stories. Let Phillip have his Emma. She herself had better things to do than sit around pining for any man!

Then they were in a bedroom and Bryn was kissing her, arousing an immediate and almost feverish response. Her head was whirling, her mind incapable of controlling the tremoring reaction of her body to the skilful caresses—of voicing even the faintest of protests as he divested her of her clothing before taking off his own clothes to join her on the bed where he had laid her.

She had never been with a naked man before, and he felt wonderful. Pure instinct guided her to respond to his lead, moulding her limbs about him, lending her lips a sensuality that drove him wild. The scent of him filled her nostrils, the salty taste of his skin spurring her to ever greater abandonment. Why should she care about Phillip? Emma could have him! She only wanted this man whose name she couldn't quite remember at the moment: this wonderful man who made her feel the way she had never felt about anyone else in her life!

The pain when he took her was fleeting enough not to matter, although he seemed to go rigid for a moment before continuing the fierce thrusting motion her whole body craved. Fulfilment came like some great crashing wave, draining her of every ounce of life force as it ebbed and leaving her shattered and quiescent beneath the suddenly smothering weight.

His inertia lasted bare seconds before he thrust himself up on to his elbows to look down at her with an expression she found disturbing.

'Why the devil didn't you tell me you were a virgin?' he demanded. 'You gave every impression of knowing what it was all about!'

'I do know what it's all about,' she said, still too drunk to care. 'Now! Can we do it again?'

With her hair tumbled about her face, and most of the make-up removed, she had a vulnerability hitherto missing. Eyes narrowed, he said, 'Just how old are you?'

'As old as my tongue and a little bit older than my teeth,' she told him smartly, then ruined it with a girlish giggle.

Bryn swore softly under his breath, and rolled away from her to sit up and reach for the clothing he had so recently discarded.

'Get dressed,' he commanded harshly. 'You're going home.'

Her head reeled along with the room when she attempted to rise. She had to fight to contain the sudden nausea. 'I...can't,' she whimpered. 'I have to lie down.'

He caught her before she could collapse back into the pillows, his mouth set grimly as he threw back the bed-clothes and drew her to a seat on the bed edge. He was wearing nothing more than briefs himself. Even in the state she was, Lian couldn't help but notice the way the light outlined the muscles in his shoulders.

Nausea swept her again. She clutched at him, face whitening. 'I think I'm going to be sick!'

Tugging a sheet from the bed, he wrapped it about her before half carrying her across to the en-suite bathroom. He even supported her head while she was ill. What seemed like an age later, she found herself being carried back to the bed and laid down still wrapped in the sheet—felt a hand smoothing back the damp hair from her face with unexpected gentleness.

'Just keep still for a while,' he said quietly. 'It will wear off.'

It took time. Closing her eyes was like going down a roller-coaster; she had to open them again or have the nausea return. When she finally summoned the strength to raise her head from the pillows, Bryn was sitting, fully dressed, in a nearby chair, a closed expression on his face.

'Feeling any better?' he asked.

Lian started to nod, and abruptly desisted. Her head felt as if it might fall off if she moved it at all, though at least the sickness had passed.

'What time is it?' she managed to whisper through a throat rough as sandpaper.

'Almost one-thirty,' he said. 'Were you expected home early?'

'There's no one there,' she acknowledged, thankful for that small mercy. 'Mother didn't know I was coming home for the weekend, so she made her own plans.' Phillip, she reflected painfully, had been swift to take advantage of her availability. His invitation had seemed like manna from heaven at the time. How dumb could anyone get?

'Home from where?' Bryn insisted.

'University. I'm reading History at Oxford.'

'So you're what—nineteen?'

'Yes.' Only just, she could have added, but refrained. Things were bad enough already. She couldn't bring herself to look at the man who had made love to her not two hours ago. She didn't even know who he was. Not in any real sense. Neither did she want to know. All she wanted right now was to go home and forget this whole sordid episode.

Except that it hadn't been sordid, had it? came the unbidden thought. Drunk or not, she could still recall the delirious pleasure of those moments she had spent in his arms. The first time was never very good for the girl, she had often heard it said. Well, that was one thing she could dispute with authority. It all depended on the man.

Hardly the point though, was it? she asked herself hollowly. She had gone to bed with a total stranger; that made her cheaper than the cheap.

'The fault is mine,' Bryn claimed, watching her changing expression. 'I should have known better than to take anything at face-value this day and age.' He got to his feet, tall, lean and darkly enigmatic. 'If you're feeling up to it, you'd better get dressed. I'll wait for you by the lifts.'

Lian waited until the outer door had closed behind him before forcing her limbs into constructive movement. She felt as weak as a kitten, with a thumping headache and a sense that nothing would ever be quite the same again. She would have welcomed a warm shower, but settled instead for a cold rinse of face and neck under the basin tap. Her eye make-up had smudged into two dark lines under her lids. With some difficulty, she wiped it off on a tissue, then used the silver-backed hairbrush laid ready on the glass shelf to bring some order to her tousled locks, making sure to remove any loose hairs from among the bristles before putting it back where she had found it.

The toilet goods laid out for use were all from an up-market range with purely masculine connotations. But then they would be, wouldn't they? Bryn was neither poor nor effeminate. Most certainly not the last. She could still see him in her mind's eye: so strong and supple, so utterly and totally the man in charge.

The muscles of her inner thighs went into involuntary spasm, sending a wave of tremoring sensation along her spine. She wanted to be with him again, she realised in shame. Didn't she have any morals left at all?

He was seated on the small sofa placed for the purpose in front of the lifts when she eventually found her way along the corridor. She didn't lift her eyes far enough to gauge his expression, but she could sense his detachment from her as he rose to press the button.

'Just put me in a taxi,' she said tonelessly. 'I'd rather go home alone.'

'To an empty house?' he asked.

'It would be that, anyway,' she pointed out. 'I just want to be on my own.'

The dark head inclined. 'Your choice.'

There were people still in the lobby. No one paid any attention to the two of them as they made their way to the main doors. Bryn held up a staying hand to the taxi-driver who had just deposited a party and was about to draw away, moving forward to open the rear door and usher Lian inside. A note was thrust into her hand, her fingers closed over it before she could draw breath to protest.

'Take care,' he said roughly, then the door was closed again and he was retreating into the hotel—out of her life.

Lian was immersed in her studies, so that first missed period was ignored—or perhaps blanked out; she could never be sure. Her attempt to put the early morning sickness down to something she had eaten was less successful. By the end of the sixth week she could no longer close either eyes or mind to what was happening to her.

The one friend in whom she confided was both sympathetic and realistic. Her mother was simply horrified that such a thing could have happened to the daughter who had been brought up to know better.

'Who is he?' she raged. 'One of your student friends? He'll have to contribute!'

'To what?' asked Lian, viewing her remaining parent without emotion.

'The abortion, of course.' Felicity Downing eyed her with drawn brows when she failed to respond. 'You're not even considering having it, I hope!'

'I'm not considering anything else,' Lian responded. 'The one thing I haven't decided about is adoption afterwards.'

Her mother's carefully cultivated refinement momentarily deserted her. 'You can't have it!' she screeched. 'What will everyone think?'

'That I made the same mistake others before me have made,' Lian came back stolidly. 'I'll naturally have to leave university—at least for the time being. I may be able to resume my courses next year after it's all over. In the meantime, I—— '

'In the meantime, you'll have to find somewhere else to stay,' declared the other with grim determination. 'There's no way I'm having you round this house with everyone pointing the finger. What about the father? Can't the two of you get married?'

'I don't want to marry him.' Lian's tone was flat. 'Nor does he want to marry me.'

'He has to bear some responsibility. Tell me his name and I'll put the whole matter in John Rawling's hands. He'll be discreet.'

Lian shook her head. 'No solicitors, thanks. And no names either. I have to see it through on my own.'

Her mother's beautifully painted mouth went tight. 'Then you'll have to do just that, I'm afraid. I'm not going to be made a laughing-stock because you were silly enough to get yourself pregnant! There are homes for unmarried mothers. You can go to one of those. Hopefully, you'll at least have the sense to sign the adoption papers when the time comes.'

Not entirely unexpected, thought Lian painfully as the other stalked from the room. They had never been as close as mother and daughter should be, and since her father had died the rift seemed to have grown wider. At forty-five, her mother was still an extremely attractive woman, with a leaning towards slightly younger men. Having a daughter at university didn't exactly help the image she liked to put across. Leaving home would be no great wrench; they were probably better apart. The problem was going to be finding a sanctuary where she could have her baby and sort out her life anew.

But she had found it, Lian thought now, five years later, gazing blindly through the long window at the inner garden below. The commune had been both home and solace during those long months of waiting. It had been at her new-found friends' advice that she had put off the decision over adoption until after the baby was born—a decision she had found no difficulty at all in making once she held the tiny dark-haired bundle in her arms. Life hadn't been easy, but there wasn't a single day when she had regretted keeping Jonathan.

And now she had found his father, things were going to be even better. She was asking for nothing to which Jonathan didn't have a right. The knowledge of his existence must have come as a shock to Bryn, but he could well afford to take care of his son.

Behind her, the door opened again to admit the subject of her thoughts. The five years had made only minor changes in the way he looked, she reflected, seeing him for the first time with the light full on his face: there was just the faintest flecking of grey at his temples, a slight deepening of the twin lines running from nose to mouth. To all intents and purposes, it was the same face she had seen in such intimate close-up that night—the same mouth that had kissed her with such memorable passion.

She threw off the intruding memories with an effort, breath suspended as she waited for what he had to say.

He remained where he was for the moment, his back to the door, expression difficult to read.

'I've been down to see your son,' he said at length. 'He's quite a character.'

'Like his father before him,' Lian returned evenly. 'He's *your* son too. Make no mistake about it.'

'Considering his looks, I can hardly deny it any further,' came the wry response. 'Mrs Banks was moved to comment on the likeness herself.'

'You mean she already guessed?'

His smile held a certain irony. 'You arrive here dragging a small boy in your wake, and refuse to leave without seeing me—what do you think? It would take an idiot not to add two and two together and come up with the right answer. The question now is what we're going to do about it.' He held up a staying hand as she made to speak. 'Yes, I know all about what *you* have in mind. Only it isn't quite as simple as you made out.' There was a pause, a change of tone. 'I think first of all we'll have lunch. That will give us the afternoon to get to grips with the detail. I told Mrs Banks to take Jonathan for a quick wash and brush-up before bringing him to the dining-room. My mother will be joining us there.'

Green eyes widened a fraction. 'Your mother?'

'She'll naturally have to know. I can hardly keep something of this nature from her.'

'But won't she be...upset?'

'I dare say. Most women would be upset to realise they have a four-year-old grandchild they didn't even know about. She's a very resilient lady. She'll adjust pretty quickly once the situation is explained to her.'

'You're going to tell her everything?' Lian was horror-struck.

'How else do I get round the facts of the matter?' he asked sardonically. 'I'll be the one to bear the brunt of reproof. You were the innocent child I seduced.' He gave her no time to reply—if there was a reply to that sally—opening the door again to indicate they leave together. 'Did you want to wash your hands before eating?'

'I could certainly do with spending a penny,' she returned with deliberation, and saw his lip slant again.

'One euphemism is as good as another. I'll show you the way. You might get lost if I leave you to your own devices.'

The corridor outside opened on to an upper hallway some short distance along. A further corridor ran off it, while to the rear a flight of stairs half concealed behind velvet curtains led down to the lower regions.

'The family quarters are on this floor and immediately below,' Bryn explained. 'The rest of the house is purely for show during the open season.'

'Why?' asked Lian curiously. 'I mean, why spend so much money just to give the public the run of the place?'

'Preservation is one thing, maintenance another.' He dismissed the subject with a shake of his head. 'By the way—our interests lie along other paths.'

The 'our' was something of a reassurance. Whatever his faults, Bryn Thornley recognised an obligation when he was faced with it. Not that it would need a whole afternoon to sort out an arrangement. Something along the lines she had already suggested would be more than acceptable.

The cloakroom to which he showed her was almost as large as her complete living area at the flat. There was even a chaise-longue covered in a silky material that matched the wall-hangings.

Washing her hands at one of the inset onyx bowls, Lian studied her reflection through the flatteringly tinted mirror and wondered if Bryn really remembered their time together. There was little enough trace of the girl he had taken to bed that night. These days, she wore the minimum of make-up, and washed and blow-dried her hair herself. The green linen suit she was wearing was a left-over from the old days, while her pale cream blouse had been picked up for next to nothing at a 'bring and buy'.

Shoes were one of the biggest problems. Jonathan grew out of them so fast, and needed proper fitting each time. Her own low-heeled pumps were from a chain store, as was the matching shoulder-bag. She'd had both three years.

At least she looked neat and tidy. Meeting Mrs Thornley was going to be enough of an ordeal without worrying about her appearance.

Bryn was waiting for her outside. From somewhere she found the ability to raise a faint smile as she joined him. 'Forward unto the breach!'

'Not all that appropriate,' he countered drily. 'I'm putting up no resistance.'

Not outwardly, she thought, but there was something in the grey eyes that threatened her peace of mind.

The dining-room overlooked the same view she had seen from the upper floor. Laid without benefit of cloth, the long mahogany table had places set for four. The

woman already seated at the head was regal in
appearance, her white hair blue-rinsed, her bosom stat-
uesque under its covering of blue silk.

'I hadn't realised we were expecting guests,' she said
pleasantly enough.

'This is Lian Downing, Mother,' replied her son. 'In
a moment or two you'll be meeting Jonathan. He's
four...' his lips twitched briefly '...and a half. That
last is very important, he tells me.' There was scarcely
a pause. 'Before he does get here, you should know he's
your grandchild.'

Great though the shock must have been, the woman
absorbed it with only the faintest tensing of facial muscle.
The gaze coming to rest on Lian's face was shorn of all
expression. 'Am I to take it you're the mother?'

Lian's chin was up and jutting, her mettle ready for
the fray. 'Yes, I am.'

'Then you'd better sit down and tell me about it.'

Bryn moved to pull out the chair on his mother's right,
sliding it beneath Lian before going round to take the
opposite seat. His eyes met hers across the width of the
table, the challenge unmistakable. 'Your party' was the
message.

She began with what coolness she could muster, aware
that Jonathan would be coming through the door any
minute now. 'I don't think it's necessary to go into any
great detail, Mrs Thornley. The fact that I had Bryn's
child tends to speak for itself, wouldn't you say?' She
didn't wait for any answer. 'I'm not here to cause trouble
for anyone. All I want is for Jonathan to be taken care
of.'

The other's brows lifted a fraction. 'You mean you
want to leave him here?'

'No!' Lian caught a hold of herself, forcibly calming her tone again. 'I didn't put that very well. When I said taken care of, I simply meant financially.'

'Miss Downing doesn't consider she can give him all the things he should have,' put in Bryn on a note which brought a spark to Lian's eyes. 'As my son, that is.'

'As anyone's son!' she shot at him. 'It's natural to want the best for one's children. I'm no exception.'

'Oh, I'd say you were exceptional in several ways,' he returned. 'How many would have had the temerity to do what you've done this morning alone? If Jonathan takes after you at all he should prove an eventual handful.'

'Stop needling the girl, Bryn,' commanded his mother. 'If you're responsible for this situation, then you should be ashamed of yourself.'

'It wasn't his fault,' Lian defended without volition, and was unable to stop the tidal flush as she caught his ironic glance. 'Not wholly,' she added. 'Anyway, it doesn't really matter now who was at fault. Jonathan is a fact. He——'

She broke off what she had been about to say as the door opened to admit both her son and the housekeeper. The latter was smiling, her whole demeanour altered from that Lian had encountered earlier.

'There's your mummy, Jonathan,' she said, releasing the boy's hand. 'Go and sit down now, and enjoy your lunch.'

Diminutive but by no means diminished, he came forward to slide into the seat at Lian's side, eyeing first the man across the table and then the woman at the head of it with candid interest. With his hair brushed back from his face, the resemblance to his father was even

more marked. Lian heard the older woman draw in a
sudden breath as if struck a blow to the solar plexus.

'I'm having a lovely time,' he announced politely, 'but
when can we go to see the animals?'

'Right after we've eaten,' promised Bryn before Lian
could speak. 'I'll take you myself.'

'Mummy, too?'

'Of course.'

Conversation lapsed while a young woman wearing a
neat grey uniform served them a first course of a beautifully prepared melon and grapefruit cocktail. Bryn got
up to fill Lian's wine glass from the decanter left to hand;
she caught the faint, emotive scent of aftershave as he
stood at the side of her chair, and felt the years slide
away again. A creature of habit—or simply a man hard
to please? Yet why not? She'd always used one particular perfume herself in the days when she could afford
it.

Mrs Thornley took it upon herself to draw Jonathan
out while they ate. Not that he needed too much
prompting to talk. Shutting him up was the problem.
Watching him handle the cocktail, Lian could only be
thankful that his table manners were up to scratch. She'd
always insisted on treating a meal as an occasion, even
when it consisted of nothing more than beans on toast.
Few things fazed him, though he could be as naughty
as the next child when the mood took him. Hopefully,
he'd remain on his best behaviour today.

Bryn watched him too—when he wasn't looking at
her. What he was thinking and feeling she had no idea,
but the sense of misgiving was still there. She had taken

it for granted that he would be only too relieved to get off so lightly, yet his attitude up to now hardly bore out that theory. Coming here might have been a mistake after all.

CHAPTER THREE

THE following dish of freshly cooked salmon called for a little assistance with Jonathan's portion in order to make sure there were no bones left hidden in the succulent flesh. Regardless of the whys and wherefores, Lian enjoyed every mouthful of her own serving, and of the light-as-a-feather raspberry mouse after it. It had been a long time since she had last sat down to a meal prepared by other people.

'I think it might be a good idea if we had a few minutes alone together before you take our guests over to the farm, Bryn,' said Mrs Thornley with obvious intent when they rose from the table after coffee. 'I'm sure Miss Downing won't mind waiting.'

His shrug was easy. 'As soon now as later, I suppose.' To Jonathan he added, 'Why don't you take your mother outside in the sunshine and wait for me? You can use the doors over there.'

Never loath to explore, Jonathan nodded assent and took Lian's hand. 'Come on, Mummy.'

The french doors in question opened on to a wide terrace, which in turn gave access via a flight of stone steps to the formal gardens below. Padded loungers were set about a small ornate pool in which goldfish could be seen swimming.

Lian sank to a seat on the raised pool edge to dabble a hand in the cool water and try to regain some self-assurance. Nothing was turning out quite as anticipated—although that shouldn't be so surprising considering the lack of precedent by which to set a standard. If anything, she should be grateful that Bryn hadn't seen fit to show her the door forthwith. In the eyes of the law she probably didn't have a leg to stand on after all this time. As a man of intelligence, he would certainly have realised that for himself.

In actual fact, the whole idea of turning up here out of the blue this way had been unrealistic. Seeing that photograph had put her in a frame of mind where nothing else had mattered but following through. Only now, having met Bryn face to face again, were the doubts beginning to materialise. She hadn't known him then, and she couldn't fathom him now. All she did know was that he set her on edge.

Jonathan had ventured down the steps and was looking at something in the grass. The Great Dane which appeared out of nowhere was so big it looked like a horse towering over him. Lian leapt to her feet in alarm, her mind already visualising the small body picked up and shaken like a rat. Undaunted by the animal's size, Jonathan greeted it with delight.

'A donkey, Mummy!' he cried. 'Come and see!'

By the time she reached the spot, the pair of them were slobbering all over each other. The dog, Lian had to admit, seemed totally without aggression. Not much more than a puppy itself, she judged, as the animal launched itself joyfully in her direction, black coat glinting in the sunlight. She made a futile attempt to ward off the over-enthusiastic welcome, lost her balance and finished up sitting on the step at her back with the big wet tongue lapping every inch of bare skin it could find.

She was too helpless with laughter to push the dog away. Dancing round yelling with delight himself,

Jonathan was no help at all. It took the sharp command from the top of the steps to break things up. Exuberance suddenly curbed, the animal dropped back on his haunches, though there was nothing cowed about the bright gaze fixed on the man descending to join them.

'Sorry about that,' said Bryn. 'He's not supposed to be in this part of the grounds.' He helped Lian to her feet. 'Are you all right?'

'No harm done,' she assured him, dusting herself down. 'What's his name?'

A smile briefly flicked his lips. 'Samson. Sam for short.' He made a gesture of dissent as the dog made to rise at the sound of his name. 'Stay! I'll get someone to take him back to his own patch,' he added. 'Obviously the gate was left open.'

For which that same someone was going to be given a rocket, Lian surmised from his tone. She could still feel the firm pressure of his fingers under her elbow, and was aware of her increased pulse-rate. He was too close for comfort even now.

'I'd like to play with him,' piped up Jonathan, patting the huge head lowered to him. 'Can I, please?'

'May I,' corrected Lian automatically. 'And I thought you wanted to see the other animals at the farm.'

'How about the three of us take Sam back to where he belongs, and then go to the farm?' suggested Bryn as the child's face registered conflict. 'You can see him again later, if you like.'

'We have a coach to catch,' said Lian a little too sharply, and received a level glance.

'There's plenty of time yet. My mother expects you back for tea.'

Jonathan had moved on ahead with Samson, one arm stretched up to the dog's collar. Lian fell into step as

Bryn moved after the pair. She wasn't sure how she felt about the invitation—if that indeed was what it was. Her plans had gone no further than convincing Bryn of his parenthood.

'Your mother must be a very unusual person to take something like this so much in her stride,' she said. 'Unless she's become shock-proof where you're concerned, that is.'

'If that's an oblique way of asking if I have other off-spring dotted around, the answer is no,' he returned. 'I never make the same mistake twice.'

'Lucky you.' She made no effort to conceal the sarcasm. 'It must be wonderful to be so sure of oneself!'

'More a case of once bitten, twice shy.' There was a harder note to his voice. 'I wasn't proud of my prowess that night, believe me. Discovering how young you really were came as a shock I could well have done without. If you hadn't been so insistent on going home alone I'd at least have known where you lived. It was only after-wards that I realised the possibilities.'

'You could have found me,' she said, 'if you'd really wanted to.'

'What makes you so sure I didn't try? All I had was a first name. No one I asked seemed to know who you were.'

There was only Phillip who *had* known, Lian conceded. She stole a glance at the hard-edged profile, wondering if he was telling the truth. 'What would you have done anyway?' she demanded. 'Offered to pay for an abortion?'

They had traversed the full length of the terrace to pass through a gate set within a high stone wall. Bryn paused in his stride to take her arm and turn her sharply towards him. His face was set in lines she found distinctly disturbing.

'Let's have one thing straight,' he clipped. 'I'm offering no excuses for what happened five years ago. Your turning up here with my son is taking some getting used to, so I'd be grateful if you'd cut out the snide comments. It isn't helping the situation.'

He was right, Lian acknowledged. It was five years too late to start casting aspersions. All the same, she refused to apologise for it. There was something about this man that made her uptight. He was too much of everything.

Jonathan broke the momentary deadlock with a shout. He had gone on ahead, still holding the dog's collar, and was now standing looking back in obvious impatience.

Bryn released her, and indicated that they proceed on their way with a curt inclination of his head. Lian briefly regretted her failure to keep matters on a businesslike footing. It was a mistake she wouldn't be making again.

Samson had a kennel and enclosed run the size of a small garden. He was kept in there only on open days, Bryn advised, firmly closing the gate on the animal. Other times he had more or less the run of the place.

It took them a further ten minutes to walk over to the farm via a route which led past what used to be the old coach house and stables. The former had been converted into a small café serving drinks and snacks to visitors. They were still arriving by the car-load. Revedon was obviously a popular destination for many a weekend outing.

Jonathan was entranced by the children's corner at the farm. Enclosed within a grassy area reached by a stile over a solid wooden fence were a dozen or more rabbits of various breeds, an equal number of guinea pigs, a couple of goat kids and the young fawn their friend on the bus had spoken of. The latter was an obvious favourite with most of the young children at present in the pasture. Quite unafraid, the animal allowed itself to be patted and petted by as many hands as could reach its red-brown, still faintly dappled coat.

'The mother broke a leg and had to be put down,' Bryn explained as he and Lian watched over the fence while Jonathan joined the little sea of admirers. 'She's been hand-reared, so she's more used to human scent than her own kind.'

'What will happen to her when she gets too big for this kind of thing?' asked Lian. 'Always assuming you don't keep deer just for show, that is.'

'You're right, we don't.' He said it without emotion. 'There's a growing demand for top-grade venison. As to Fancy here, she'll probably go to a zoo when the time comes. At full size, she'd be capable of causing injury to a child just by being playful.'

'A good thing Jonathan doesn't know,' she commented. 'He'd want to take her home with him. Hardly the kind of pet you could keep in a flat.'

His smile was perfunctory. 'I don't imagine there are all that many pets you *could* keep in a flat.'

'He has a couple of gerbils,' she defended. 'They don't cost much to feed, and a neighbour made him the cage.'

'It wasn't a criticism,' he came back. 'As a matter of fact, I think you've done a very good job on such limited resources. He doesn't come across as deprived of anything.'

Except security, she thought, and she was the only one capable as yet of feeling that particular lack.

Moving to allow more room for another fond parent to view proceedings, she felt her arm come into contact with the muscular one next to her, the ensuing tingle penetrating the material of her sleeve as if her skin were bared to the touch. Of the other couples standing around the fence, they were the only ones not giving off that aura of belonging which went hand in glove with the marital state—at least, to her it did.

'You said you hadn't seen your mother in five years,' Bryn remarked, apparently unaware of her reactions to his closeness as he made no move to draw away. 'Does that mean she refused you any financial help?'

'It means,' Lian answered, 'that I refused to ask for it.'

'Pride—or simple retaliation?'

He was too astute by half, came the wry acknowledgement. Chin jutting, she said flatly, 'If she'd cared at all she'd have said to hell with everyone else in the first place.'

'In a perfect world, we'd all be flawless,' came the dry reply. 'Don't judge too harshly.'

'You don't know her,' she retorted. 'I do—or did. And she isn't what I came here to discuss.'

'True,' he agreed. 'And we still have to come to an arrangement. Naturally it will have to be more than just verbal.'

'You mean a legal agreement?'

'Of course.'

Better by far if the whole affair was organised impersonally from here-on-in, Lian had to agree, yet couldn't deny the sudden hollowness in the pit of her stomach.

'I really think we'll have to pass up tea with your mother,' she said shortly. 'The coach we came up on leaves at six on the dot, and we still have to get back to Kendal.'

'I'll be driving you back home,' he declared. 'So you don't need worry about the time. It's only an hour or so by car.'

Lian straightened away from the fence, her face set. 'Thanks, but no, thanks. We got here under our own steam, we'll go back the same way.'

He had turned with her, expression equally unyielding. 'I can't allow that.'

Her indrawn breath was no sham. *'Can't?'*

'Won't, then, if we're being pedantic about it.' He took her arm as she opened her mouth to tell him what he could do with his decrees, drawing her out of immediate range of nearby ears. Grey eyes held green relentlessly. 'You can't have everything your own way. If I'm involved at all, then I'm going to have some say in what goes. We'll have tea, then I'll drive you home. All right?'

'No, it isn't all right!' She was trembling with a mixture of anger and some other emotion she didn't want to define. 'You might be able to walk roughshod over your employees, but you're not doing it with me! I don't want to be driven back. We have return tickets, and I intend using them.'

There was no give in the set of his jaw, nor in the firm pressure of the fingers still wrapped about her arm. His gaze dropped to her mouth, lingering there for an interminable moment before moving on down to the hollow of her throat exposed beneath the open collar of her blouse to take in the pulse fluttering beneath the skin. She had a feeling that if they'd been anywhere but where they were he would have pulled her to him and expressed his own anger with devastating force—a result for which she wasn't looking and certainly wouldn't have liked. To have known his kisses once was enough.

'Mummy?' Unnoticed by either of them, Jonathan had climbed back over the stile and was watching them now from a short distance away with bright-eyed curiosity. 'Can I go and play with Sam again?'

Bryn was the first to regain full control of himself. Features relaxing, he said, 'If that's what you want to do, we'll make tracks.' The glance he turned back to Lian held a challenge. 'Right?'

Short of defying him to do his worst in front of Jonathan and everyone else on the scene, there was nothing she could do but go along. She bottled up her tight-throated fury to summon a smile for her son. 'Not for too long, though. We have a long way to go home.'

Bryn waited until they were on their way, with Jonathan far enough ahead not to overhear before making any comment. 'You don't,' he observed, 'give up easily.'

'Not to overbearance,' she returned on a frosty note.

'You came to me,' he pointed out. 'That gives me some licence. I've no intention of allowing you to make that return journey by coach, Lian, so you may as well reconcile yourself to it. If I have to use physical force to get you into the car when the time comes, I'll do that too.'

She believed him. Not that it helped her to accept the situation. She didn't want him taking them home because she didn't want him to know where they lived, yet that was ridiculous because the address would have to be disclosed eventually. Coming here had definitely been a mistake; she could feel it in her bones. Bryn wasn't going to be content to leave everything in the hands of his lawyers.

They made it back to the house in near silence after that, picking up Samson from his kennel on the way. The afternoon had turned beautiful after the early threat of rain, the sky cleared of all but a few wisps of cloud. Mrs Thornley was sitting out on the terrace along with a young woman around Lian's own age whose dark hair and clear-cut features were all too indicative of her family status.

'Hi there,' greeted the latter pleasantly as the four of them came up the steps. 'Had a nice walk?'

'Fine.' Bryn's regard went from her to his mother, who nodded, and back again. 'Lian, I'd like you to meet my sister, Fiona.'

Somewhat at a loss, Lian managed an acknowledgement. There had been no mention of a sister before this. On the other hand, she supposed there had been no particular reason for mention to be made. That the other knew the facts of her own role was only too apparent. Yet there was no censure in the eyes so like Bryn's own.

'And this is Jonathan, of course,' she said, smiling at the boy. 'Supposing you and I go and find some lemonade?'

'Sam too?' he asked.

'Sam too.'

He considered for a brief moment, then nodded. 'OK.'

'Yes, thank you,' Lian corrected, warming to the other girl. She added with sincerity. 'It's nice of you to take the trouble.'

'All in the family,' came the blithe comment, drawing a sudden glint to her brother's eyes. 'Come along, both of you.'

Boy and dog moved as one, the latter towering over the former. There was a pause after the little party disappeared indoors. Mrs Thornley was the first to break the silence.

'Come and sit down,' she invited Lian. 'Tea won't be here for another half-hour yet.'

With Jonathan gone, there was no point in putting her case for a premature departure, Lian conceded. She took the indicated seat, while Bryn perched himself comfortably on the pool side.

'You'll agree that the child's interests have to come before any other consideration,' remarked the older woman without preamble. 'He's the innocent in this affair.'

'It's only for his sake that I'm here at all,' Lian returned with surprising equability. 'I don't want anything for myself.'

There was a certain scepticism in the other's regard. 'I seem to have heard that claim before.'

'Except in my case, it happens to be true.' Lian was determined not to let herself be rattled. 'I can't be held responsible for other people, Mrs Thornley.'

'You're certainly not without spirit.' The comment held a somewhat grudging approval. 'What exactly are your plans for Jonathan's future?'

'The same as any mother's,' Lian returned. 'I want him to have a good education, to grow up with a balanced outlook on life, to have a career instead of being stuck in some dead-end job that wouldn't fulfil him.'

'But still minus a father.' It was a statement not a question, the tone matter-of-fact. 'A boy needs a man about the house. I gather you have no one in mind to fill that gap?'

'Lian's been too busy bringing up our son to find herself a boyfriend,' put in Bryn levelly. 'No inquisition, we agreed earlier. It will all be sorted out.'

He was too close again, Lian decided as he rested an elbow on the arm of her chair: too close and too overpowering. She knew he was studying her face, but nothing would have persuaded her to turn her head. Her heart was thudding against her ribcage, her every sense tuned to the memory of how it had been that long-ago night. It hadn't been easy these past years sublimating that awakened sensuality; there were times when she longed for some release from her self-imposed celibacy. If she'd known how being with Bryn again would affect her, she'd have thought twice before making the decision to come. It was a complication she could well do without.

Fiona's return, trailing Jonathan and Sam in her wake, was a relief.

'Cook says if that animal comes into her kitchen again she's leaving,' announced the former cheerfully. 'I suppose one can see her point. He just cleaned up a bowl of egg custard while we weren't looking.'

'He was hungry,' defended Jonathan. 'He didn't know it wasn't to eat.'

'No harm done,' Bryn assured him. 'Cook's been threatening to leave for the past twenty years, but she's still here.' He got to his feet, easing muscles cramped by the position he had been occupying. 'A phone call I need to make.'

To his solicitor? Lian wondered. It hardly seemed likely on a Saturday afternoon, but with these people who could tell? Watching Jonathan playing set and catch with the big dog, she knew a serious regret for having introduced him to all this. Luckily children soon forgot. Once back home, he would be content with his gerbils and his goldfish.

Fiona came to take Bryn's place on the pool side. 'He's a super kid,' she declared. 'Bright, without being

precocious. The only other child I know his age is as
spoiled a little brat as they come. Belongs to some
friends, which makes it doubly difficult to administer a
swift slap in the right place at the right time. Maybe if
they saw Jonathan, they'd realise where they went
wrong.'

Lian laughed, relaxing to the other's casual manner.
'It's difficult sometimes to know where to draw the line.
I've been lucky.'

'I'd say it took rather more than luck. He has Bryn's
character, for certain. You should have seen the way he
faced up to Cook when she said all animals should be
put down. I'm not sure he knew exactly what she meant,
but he certainly got the gist. The woman's a real Tartar,
yet she was the one who finished up backing down.' She
dropped her voice a little, not exactly excluding her
mother but addressing her remarks on a purely personal
level. 'It must have taken a lot of courage to do what
you've done. Given the same circumstances, I'd have
taken the easy way out.'

'Given the same circumstances, you don't know what
you might be capable of,' Lian rejoined. 'I've surprised
myself at times.' She stirred restlessly, glancing at the
watch that had been a birthday present the year her father
had died. 'I never intended staying this length of time.'

It was Fiona's turn to laugh. 'You surely didn't imagine
you could drop a bombshell like this one and just walk
straight out again? Whatever else my brother might or
might not be, a side-stepper he isn't. He'll assume his
responsibilities the way a man should—if all too rarely
does.'

Lian said softly. 'Only up to a point. The last thing
Jonathan needs is an honorary guardian.'

'Hardly honorary anything. He's his father. He may even decide to legalise the position.'

Over her dead body, Lian thought, feeling her stomach lurch.

Bryn came out again from the house in the wake of the tea-trolley pushed by a young maid. There was apparently no staff shortage at Revedon. Poured by Mrs Thornley herself into Spode china cups, the tea was hot and fragrant and refreshing. Very different from the pottery mugs and supermarket brand to which she was more accustomed, Lian was bound to acknowledge.

There were no cucumber sandwiches, just freshly baked scones and small, fancy cakes for those who wanted them. Apart from Jonathan, no one, it seemed, did. The staff would finish up the left-overs, Lian assumed, and stifled a momentary temptation to ask for a doggy bag. Humour of that kind would probably not be appreciated.

Sitting in the warmth of the July afternoon, listening to the conversation which by unspoken consent excluded any further mention of her reason for being here, she allowed her gaze to rove across the far trees to the line of distant hills. Somewhere over there was Windermere, which they wouldn't now be visiting. Not that Jonathan showed any sign of missing that particular experience, it was true, but he might remember the promise tomorrow.

Tomorrow was going to seem an anticlimax in more ways than the one. Perhaps she would have been better leaving the trip until the Sunday after all, with work to take her mind off things the following morning. If Fiona was only halfway right about her brother, there were going to be unforeseen problems ahead. Only no way would Bryn be allowed to take more than a peripheral interest in Jonathan's welfare. She was his mother; her rights were paramount.

It was gone four-thirty before Bryn made any move towards getting them home. Jonathan was loath to leave his friend, but seemed to accept it after his father spoke quietly with him. Neither Mrs Thornley nor Fiona said a great deal by way of farewell. Lian guessed they were finding the departure as awkward as she was herself.

Belted into the front passenger seat of the black XJ40, with Jonathan already nodding in the back, she made one more attempt to regain the initiative.

'We're still in time for the coach. If you just drop us off in Kendal...'

'I'm taking you all the way.' Bryn's tone was obdurate. 'Sit back and relax.'

She sat back, but not to relax. An hour was a long time—how long she was only just beginning to realise. And at the end of it? She could scarcely dispatch him back to Revedon without offering him a coffee at the very least, which meant inviting him into their home.

Why hadn't she left well alone while she'd had the chance? she thought hollowly. She had an awful feeling that nothing was ever going to be the same again.

There were still visitors loose in the grounds. Closing time was six o'clock, Bryn advised. Leaving the estate via the same entrance used by the bus that morning, he bypassed Kendal altogether to get on to the M6, settling down to a steady, almost soothing seventy as if mindful of the small passenger in the back.

'We'll be there well before seven,' he promised. 'Which part of Manchester, by the way?'

'Salford,' Lian answered. 'Off Adelphi Street.'

'You'll have to direct me. I'm not familiar with the area.'

Lian had always found motorway driving soporific. Today was no exception. Before they had gone twenty miles she was having to fight to keep her eyes open.

'Why don't you give in and get your head down?' suggested Bryn eventually, without appearing to even glance her way. 'I'll wake you when I need directions.'

Securely held by the rear seatbelt, Jonathan was already in the land of nod. Lian saw no sense in denying her own need. She felt emotionally if not physically drained. Bryn would get them safely home. On that score she had no doubts at all.

She slept the whole distance, awakening with a start when he said her name. For a moment she had no idea at all what was happening, then memory returned along with a sudden and overriding sense of depression as she sat up straight. With head and body cocooned by supple leather, she had developed none of the usual stiffness and neck-ache associated with sleeping in a moving vehicle. That in itself was some solace. She only hoped her mouth hadn't fallen open. There was nothing that looked worse!

'We're coming into Salford now,' said Bryn. 'Just tell me which way to turn at the junction.'

Lian did so, directing him through the back streets to the block of high-rise flats visible between the buildings. He said nothing when they eventually drew up outside. Nor did he reveal any inner judgement. Woken by the lull in motion, Jonathan sat up and yawned.

'Are we here, Mummy?'

'Yes.' She hesitated before adding for Bryn's benefit, 'I'd offer you a coffee or something, only you might come out to find all your tyres missing.'

His shrug made light of the warning. 'I'll take the risk.'

She had been afraid of that. Sliding from the car, she nodded a silent greeting to a neighbour just about to turn into the entrance of the block, before opening the rear door to let Jonathan out. Despite his long sleep, he was still too tired to walk straight. Bryn locked the car and came round to swing him up in his arms, meeting Lian's eyes with a faint lift of a brow as if expecting her to object.

'Lead the way,' he invited.

Going up in the lift, she watched the indicator with bated breath, half expecting another of the too frequent breakdowns. The sixth-floor landing was reached without incident, her key extracted from her handbag, the door opened on her own little lobby with its white-painted walls and cheery if cheap red carpet.

'Jonathan's room is along at the end,' she said. 'I think it might be a good idea if he went straight to bed, if you don't mind waiting for your coffee. It's been a long day.'

Comfortable and secure in his father's arms, the child was already asleep again. Bryn took him into the tiny bedroom and laid him gently on the narrow divan, brushing the tumbled dark hair back from the small face with a light hand before straightening.

'I'll make the coffee,' he said, 'while you see to Jonathan.' He caught the doubtful look in her eyes and tilted a lip. 'I'm capable.'

'I'll show you where the kitchen is,' she offered, taking him at his word.

'I'll find it.' He was moving as he spoke, passing her in the doorway. 'You concentrate on Jonathan.'

With only five other doors to look behind, he was hardly going to have any difficulty, Lian acknowledged wryly. She only had instant coffee in stock, but she doubted if that would faze him either. How long he planned on staying around was a question to which she didn't want to give too much thought. She hadn't planned on any of this.

CHAPTER FOUR

BRYN was standing in the living-room window looking out across the little balcony to the distant view of the Derbyshire moors when she eventually went through. She was vitally aware of the tapering line from broad shoulder to narrow waist and hip—of the muscular length of his legs beneath the well-cut trousers.

'Could be a lot worse, I suppose,' he remarked. 'Do you decorate the place yourself?'

She nodded as he turned to look at her, and sat down on the second-hand sofa she had also re-covered herself in material bought from the local market. He had made a whole pot of coffee and set out two mugs on her only tray, along with a jug of milk and a small glass dish containing sugar.

'I couldn't find a proper sugar basin,' he admitted.

'I broke the last one,' she returned, pouring from the earthenware pot. 'I didn't get round to buying a replacement. How many spoonfuls?'

'None,' he said. 'No milk either, thanks.'

He came to take a seat in the fireside chair the other side of the low table, accepting the mug she handed across to him and tasting the black liquid without comment. 'You've made a nice home here,' he stated. 'You're to be congratulated.'

'One cuts one's cloth,' she responded lightly. '*You've* made a pretty wonderful job of Revedon.'

Judging from the fleeting glint in the grey eyes, the irony didn't get past him. 'I had some help.' There was a pause, a change of tone. 'Where did you plan on eating tonight?'

Her gesture encompassed the room. 'Right here.'

'I'll rephrase,' he said drily. '*What* did you plan on eating tonight? I took a look in the refrigerator. Assuming the chops are for tomorrow...'

'I'd planned on calling in at the local fishery after we got off the coach,' she acknowledged with reluctance. 'Jonathan loves fish and chips.'

'And you?'

She shrugged, assuming indifference. 'They don't do any harm from time to time. Normally, I'd have cooked something here, but we weren't going to be home until almost nine o'clock. The refrigerator is a very old one, anyway. I don't like to risk storing meat for too long.'

'So get a new one.' He held up a staying hand before she could speak, mouth twisting. 'That was thoughtless of me.'

'Just a little.' Her colour had risen. 'Jonathan doesn't lack proper nutrition, if that's what you're intimating.'

'On the contrary, he's obviously a very healthy child.' He paused again, jawline firming. 'I think it's time we stopped skirting the subject and got down to brass tacks, don't you? Much as you've done to make this a home from home, it's no place to bring up a small boy. Where can he play, for instance?'

'There's the park.' Lian was shaken by sudden portent. 'What exactly are you suggesting?'

'He's my son,' came the level reply. 'There's no doubt in my mind about that. I naturally want what's going to be best for him.'

'You'll not get him away from me!' She was sitting bolt upright on the edge of her seat, eyes blazing like emeralds. 'I should have known better than to come to you at all!'

'But you did come, and there's no going back,' he returned inexorably. 'Revedon is his birthright. Did you really imagine I was going to settle for the kind of arrangement you had in mind? I want him.'

Somehow she got a grip on herself. 'Then you'll have to want! As his mother, I have prior claim.'

Expression controlled, he said, 'I wouldn't dispute it. So come with him.'

It took a moment or two to penetrate. When she did find her voice it was with difficulty. 'As what? Some kind of resident nanny?'

He smiled faintly. 'The position I had in mind would include that kind of duty. It's a bit late in the day for the knee-bending bit, so we'll take it as read. We can be married inside the week. Register office, naturally, but no less valid.'

This time it took Lian even longer to summon speech. Her throat hurt. 'Fiona suggested you might do something like this.'

If he was surprised he wasn't showing it. 'And what was your reaction?'

She drew in a long, steadying breath. 'The same as now. It wasn't a husband I came looking for.'

'You already made that clear. All the same, it's what I'm offering. Jonathan's of an age where he needs a father. I may not be experienced in that line, but I'm a quick study.'

The quirk of humour was too deliberate to be genuine, Lian thought. He was hating this as much as she was. She put up a distracted hand to rake back the hair from her forehead in a gesture her son, for one, would have recognised as the prelude to some last-stand declaration, and said forcibly, 'I don't want to marry you, Bryn. There has to be some other way!'

'Only adoption, if he's to have my name legally.' His mouth firmed again. 'I'll fight you for him, if necessary.'

'You've barely known him a day,' she pointed out, hanging on to the threads of her own control. 'Isn't it a bit soon to make a decision that could ruin your whole life?'

'Alter, yes, not ruin. I'm thirty-five. It's not before time I thought about settling down to some family life. Ready-made in this case, which helps. I can't say I'm all that enamoured of babies.'

Lian was silent, gazing at him helplessly. He meant every word, that was obvious. With all his resources behind him, who was to say he wouldn't win a case brought before the courts? No matter how slight, was it a risk she cared to run?

He got up after a moment, coming across to sit down at her side and take her by the shoulders, forcing her to look at him. His face was set in lines of determination.

'I've had all day to think the thing through, Lian, and it's the only realistic way to settle the matter. You didn't find me repulsive five years ago. I flatter myself I can conjure a similar response from you at the appropriate time.'

A tremor ran through her, so deep and wild he must have felt it. A smile touched his lips at the look which sprang in her eyes. 'The name-only idea is a non-starter so far as I'm concerned. You're a very attractive young woman. I'd be less than honest if I pretended that fact didn't have any bearing. As my wife, you would be expected to share my bed as well as my home. Not a lot to ask.'

His voice was lulling her, conjuring memories—disturbing memories—of another time, another place. She stiffened for a moment when he dropped his head to find her mouth, but only for a moment. It was as if the years had rolled away.

It took the feather-light touch of his fingers at her breast to jerk her back to her senses. He allowed himself to be pushed away, watching the emotions chasing across her face with enigmatic eyes.

'Not so difficult, is it?'

'It's impossible!' She was breathing fast, pulse racing, mind unable to cope with any logical trend of thought. 'We don't even . . . know each other!'

To do him credit, he didn't attempt to make anything of the double meaning inherent in that statement, although he would certainly have noted it. 'So, we learn,' he said. 'With Jonathan as incentive. Plenty of marriages start out with less.' This time the smile was less constrained. 'I could have worded that better too. What I'm trying to say is it's the only way we have of giving him the balanced family life he's entitled to. And there's no argument you can bring up that will change my mind on that score.'

The words were dragged from her. 'It seems I don't have much of a choice.'

'Not if you want to keep him, you don't.' With the battle to all intents and purposes won, he became businesslike again. 'There'll be arrangements to make. I'd suggest Wednesday. That should give you time to do what you have to do with regard to this place.'

'That's far too soon.' Lian was still too dazed to conjure any stronger protest. 'There's the furniture, for one thing, and——'

'There's nothing here you're going to need apart from the purely personal items,' Bryn returned incisively. 'I'll bring the station-wagon down. Now, about that supper. Are there any take-aways in the vicinity?'

'There's a Chinese three streets away.' She attempted to gather herself together. 'I shouldn't have thought you ever frequented such places.'

'I don't frequent discotheques either, but I know they exist.' The irony was mild. 'Put some plates to warm. I'll be back.'

Lian sat where she was for several minutes after he had left the flat. Everything felt unreal. This morning she had set out to make what she had considered a straight if not exactly simple claim, now here she was under orders to marry the man she hadn't seen in five long years.

Whatever else she had anticipated when he'd insisted on bringing them home, a proposal had been furthest from her mind—regardless of what Fiona had suggested. And Wednesday! How on earth could he expect her to prepare either herself or Jonathan for such total transfiguration of lifestyle in four days? Explaining the whys and wherefores alone was going to be difficult enough without going into detail a four-year-old could hardly be expected to take in. 'The gentleman we went to visit is your real daddy' —how would that sound? No, that part would have to be left out for the time being.

She was no nearer coming to terms with the situation when Bryn returned with the loaded carrier. He'd brought something of everything, he said, so they could have a choice. Lian had never felt less like eating in her life, yet found herself doing so anyway once the appetising aromas reached her nostrils. On a practical level, such a repast was too good to pass up.

'Feeling better?' asked Bryn over a further mug of coffee after they finished the meal.

Lian shook her head, avoiding his gaze. 'Not so you'd notice.' Her laugh was forced. 'I keep thinking I'm going to wake up any minute!'

'I'm no figment of the subconscious,' he responded drily. 'I could prove it to you, if you have doubts.'

She looked at him then, a calculated glance that took in the hint of satire in the slight curve of his lips. 'Take up where we left off, you mean?' she suggested boldly. 'That's hardly the kind of awakening I had in mind. If I agree to this . . . idea of yours——'

'You don't have a choice,' he reminded her. 'I intend having my son, whatever it takes.' The pause was brief. 'On the other hand, I might have been a bit precipitate with regard to the wedding itself. Would the week after next suit you better?'

They could have been discussing a starting date for a new job, she reflected. In effect, she supposed that was exactly what they were doing. A job with a difference in the sense that she was going to be called on to perform duties above and beyond the normal. The fact that physical intimacy would be nothing new was neither here nor there. Five years was a long time. They were two different people.

'It would give me more time to prepare Jonathan,' she agreed, and hesitated before adding, 'You don't expect me to tell him the whole truth right away, do you?'

'Children that age tend to accept things matter-of-factly. I think you might risk it.' The tone was smooth enough but with an underlying mandate. 'I don't fancy playing "uncle" to my own son.'

'He's hardly going to start calling you Daddy right away either,' Lian couldn't resist pointing out. 'That would be expecting a little too much.'

'Possibly. We shan't know till the time comes, shall we?' Bryn got to his feet, tall and lean and totally in command of the situation. 'I'd better be heading back. Mother's going to be waiting to hear the outcome.'

Lian rose too, unsurprised to find her knees shaky. 'It's going to be something of a shock for her.'

'I doubt it. Very little shocks her. If anything, she'll consider I took the only practical route.'

'For Jonathan's sake, you mean?'

'For all our sakes. We all stand to gain from the arrangement.' He stood looking across at her for a moment, mind impenetrable. 'It will work out. We just have to put the effort in, that's all. I'll phone you to-morrow, and come down again Monday to get the whole thing on the road. All right?'

Lian nodded; there seemed very little left to say. Accompanying him to the door, she wondered if there was any chance of his changing his mind again over-night—rejecting the thought almost as soon as it oc-curred because people like Bryn Thornley didn't go in for vacillation. They were going to be married, and she had better accept it. For Jonathan's sake if not for her own.

She scarcely knew whether to be relieved or sorry when he made no attempt to kiss her again. Watching him walk across the landing to the lift, she still couldn't believe it was all really happening. There would never be another day quite like this one, for sure! It went beyond all reckoning.

*   *   *

The wedding took place on a sunny Wednesday morning. Apart from the neighbour who had looked after Jonathan while Lian was at work, and the only other close friend she had allowed herself, there were no guests. Fiona had wanted to attend, but Bryn had put her off at Lian's request. Having any of his family there would have made her feel even more aware of what was lacking from this union.

Jonathan himself had received the news with far less disturbance than she could ever have anticipated. Having a daddy like other children was OK with him, even if he had had to wait until he was nearly grown-up to find him. The realisation that he was going to be seeing Samson every day overcame any doubts which might have arisen. The big dog had been all he had talked about this past week and a half.

Emerging from the register office at Bryn's side, Lian wondered when she was going to stop feeling this sense of unreality. There had been so much to do in the preceding days, she'd been carried along without thinking too much about what was to come. Getting rid of all but their personal effects had been the biggest job. In the end she had simply called in a house clearance firm and accepted the offer they made for the lot, which hadn't been much.

They'd spent last night in a hotel, at Bryn's insistence, leaving the flat to be emptied and the keys returned to the council. It had been quite a wrench saying goodbye to familiar surroundings—an even greater one to take her leave of independence. As Bryn Thornley's wife she would have a position of some import, but it was no substitute for autonomy. That was something she was only just beginning to appreciate.

'Cheer up,' Bryn murmured. 'It's all over.'

Bar the shouting, Lian added mentally, completing the localism. She had a premonition there might well be some of that to come.

Wearing new shorts and smart blue blazer bought him by his father, Jonathan looked every inch his son. Lian was glad she hadn't attempted to hide that fact from her friends, because one glimpse of the two of them together would have been enough to give her away. Seated in the rear of the Jaguar, he prattled away nineteen to the dozen about what he and Sam were going to do together, much to Bryn's amusement.

'Glad some of us have their priorities in order,' he commented *sotto voce* as they headed out on the A6. 'I'd have organised a honeymoon if I'd thought you'd appreciate the gesture.'

'I wouldn't,' Lian assured him. 'It's hardly that kind of marriage, is it?'

Dark brows lifted sardonically. 'How many kinds are there?'

'You know what I mean.' Mindful of the little ears in the back, she lightened her tone. 'What time are we expected at Revedon?'

'When we arrive.' He slanted a glance and relented a little. 'There's a nice little pub I know where we can drop off for lunch. I thought we'd go the long way round. It's more scenic.'

'Whatever you like.'

This time the glance held an element of intolerance. 'I'm laying down suggestions, not cut-and-dried decisions. You're at liberty to appeal.'

'Thanks.' She was hard put to retain the lightness. 'For the present I'm quite content to just go along.'

He was silent for some minutes after that. Not a brooding silence though, Lian was bound to concede, just a lack of anything he particularly wanted to say.

She was very much aware of his dark attraction in the grey suit and sparkling white shirt—of the power contained beneath the formal attire. Most women would regard her as fortunate indeed to be married to such a magnificent male animal. Only she wasn't most women, and this was no ordinary marriage, although tonight he would expect her to act as if it were.

A tremor ran through her at the thought of what was to come. It wouldn't be the first time she had made love with a man she didn't love, of course, but this time she wouldn't have the same amount of alcohol in her bloodstream to dull her sense of values. It wasn't the same for men; they could make love to any woman they found attractive without needing to justify the action. Liberalisation was all very well, but it didn't alter basic make-up. She needed to love and be loved to be at ease with intimacy.

The public house Bryn had spoken of lay just outside Clitheroe. There was a special area set aside for families with young children in tow. Whether he had chosen the place because of this, Lian couldn't be sure and refrained from asking. It was enough to be banned from the main bar without labouring the point.

Thriftily, she had chosen a dress and jacket in beige and white which could be worn later, and didn't look at all out of place in these surroundings. The white, floppy-brimmed hat that had been her only concession to the occasion she left in the car. They could, she thought as they ate, be any family out for a day's run. Certainly there was nothing to suggest otherwise.

'I should have ordered champagne,' said Bryn over dessert. 'It still isn't too late if you'd fancy it?'

'You're driving,' she pointed out, thankful that he hadn't drawn attention to them in that manner. She flushed a little as the expressive eyebrow flicked upwards. 'Just a comment.'

'You sounded like a wife,' he said. 'A token mouthful wouldn't have impaired my faculties to any great extent. However, I don't mind waiting to celebrate, if you don't.'

'*I'd* like some champagne,' said Jonathan, drawing a sudden appealing grin and a shake of the head.

'It gets up your nose. Best stick to orange juice for the time being.'

From the look on Jonathan's face, Lian had a feeling he was thinking the other sounded more fun, but he accepted the edict without argument. He wasn't yet quite enough at home with Bryn to treat him with the familiarity a son might accord his father, though she doubted if it would be long before they achieved that kind of rapport. Unlike many adults unaccustomed to children, Bryn didn't talk down to him. That alone had to help.

It was gone two o'clock when they got on the road again. The countryside changed character as they left Lancashire and came into Westmoreland: high rolling hills stretched away eastward to form the Pennine chain of mountains.

After Kirkby Lonsdale, they took to the back lanes, passing through secluded villages nestling beneath the high fells. There was room to breathe out here, Lian thought. She found herself looking forward to exploring her new surroundings.

Entering the Revedon estate for the second time gave her a strange feeling. If she could have imagined how the venture was going to turn out, would she have carried it through? she wondered. A question to which there was no answer, of course, and therefore it was a waste of time asking it. They were here and there was no going back. The sooner she settled her mind to that, the better for all concerned.

Bryn drove straight round to the private side-entrance, and left the car to be washed and garaged by the man in charge of that department.

The Jaguar wasn't the only vehicle on the premises. Apart from the station-wagon Bryn had driven down at the weekend to fetch the bulk of their luggage, there was a Mercedes, a Porsche, and a couple of Land Rovers Lian assumed were for use on the estate.

Mrs Thornley and Fiona were waiting for them in the large and comfortable sitting-room. Lian gained an impression of warm chintz and glowing wood, with the terrace on which they had sat the last time she was here visible through the opened french windows. Then Fiona was coming forward to put an arm about her shoulders and kiss her lightly on the cheek.

'Welcome home,' she said.

The simple greeting relieved the tension Lian was feeling in a way no other, more effusive reception could have done. She smiled back at her sister-in-law gratefully. 'Thanks.'

'You're just in time for tea,' said Mrs Thornley, already established behind the trolley. 'I told Hillary to set for five.'

'Almost where I came in,' Lian joked, and immediately regretted it because it wasn't quite the thing to say. 'I'm sorry,' she added impulsively. 'That was tasteless of me.'

'First-night nerves,' said Fiona on a bland note which earned her a reproving glance from her mother. 'You look very smart, Jonathan.'

'Thank-you-where's-Sam?' he answered all of a piece, which made everyone laugh and eased the atmosphere.

'We'll go and find him right after tea,' promised Bryn. He took a seat at Lian's side on one of the sofas, accepting the cup his mother handed him but shaking his head to her offer of a buttered scone. 'We had lunch on the way. The Red House is under new management. They've ruined the place.'

'A pity,' agreed Mrs Thornley. 'It's happening every-where. Duncan is back, incidentally, so he'll be able to sort out that problem.'

That would be Duncan Fleming, the estate controller, Lian surmised. On the boards of several companies, Bryn had little time left to manage the place himself. He was going to be around the rest of the week, he had said. After that was anyone's guess.

She let the conversation flow around her, thinking of the familiar little flat and the people she had left behind—more than half wishing she were back there right now. She couldn't imagine a time when she would be able to call this place home. It was too big, too grand, too utterly outside her experience.

Jonathan, thank heaven, was behaving in exemplary fashion. He had to find his feet in unfamiliar sur-roundings too. At least he didn't have to share a room with anyone—to say nothing of a bed. That, more than anything, was disturbing her. First-night nerves indeed!

She became aware that Fiona was speaking to her, and shook off her introspection to offer a receptive ear.

'I'll take you up to your room while Bryn and Jonathan go looking for Sam,' the other girl offered. 'You'll want to start sorting out your things.'

'Good idea,' her brother agreed. 'We'll be going out for dinner tonight, by the way.'

Lian said confusedly, 'All of us?'

'Just the bride and groom, silly,' supplied her sister-in-law without malice. 'There has to be something to mark the occasion.'

Avoiding Bryn's eyes as she got to her feet, Lian had the idea that he knew exactly what was going through her mind. Not that it would probably make any difference when it came to the event. He had warned her what he would expect from her. Why would he forgo the one advantage he stood to gain?

Jonathan was happy enough to accompany his father. Both shorn of their jackets, they went out via the french windows to drop down the terrace steps.

'Bryn's taking to fatherhood like a duck to water,' commented Fiona on the way upstairs. 'Of course, it helps having a child old enough and intelligent enough to hold a conversation with. I don't see him coo-cooing a baby.'

Lian didn't either. Immaterial at present anyway. She had no intention of getting pregnant again for a long time to come—if ever.

'Do you have a current boyfriend?' she asked, more to make conversation than through any real need to know. 'A serious one, that is.'

'It depends what you mean by serious,' came the light response. 'There's someone I see rather more of than most, but we're not contemplating marriage, or anything like it at present. Paul's good company. We have a lot of fun. To be honest,' she added, 'I'm not sure I'm cut out to be anyone's wife. Too much like putting one's head in a noose!' She caught herself up, glancing round in smiling contrition. 'You'll have noticed I'm prone to putting my foot in it.'

Lian made some suitably flippant reply, thinking the other might have a point. Total freedom of choice was a thing of the past.

The bedroom she was to share with Bryn was light and airy, the furnishings of superb quality but modern design. Thick moss-green carpeting made a background for the fresh green and white curtains and matching bed cover. One half of the room contained a suite of cane furniture to form a comfortable sitting area. There was also a large and sumptuous adjoining bathroom complete with semi-sunken bath and separate shower.

'The tub can be turned into a jacuzzi too,' Fiona advised. 'Bryn likes his creature comforts as well as the next. I thought you'd probably prefer to unpack your things yourself. You'll find everything in the larger of the two wardrobes.' She paused. 'Need any help?'

Lian shook her head. 'I'll be fine.' Impulsively, she added, 'Thanks for making me so welcome, Fiona. I realise what a shock this whole thing must have been for you—and for your mother.'

The return smile was easy. 'It could have been a bigger shock still if you'd been other than what you are. Mother would obviously have preferred a properly arranged wedding, and to have known Jonathan from the word go, but she's happy enough to have him from here-on-in.' Fiona seemed about to add something else, then apparently changed her mind. 'I'll leave you to it, then.'

'Where will Jonathan be sleeping?' Lian asked quickly.

'Two doors down on the other side of the corridor. Bryn had the room specially done up for him. Take a look, if you want to. I'll see you later.'

Left alone, Lian stood irresolute for a moment, then took Fiona at her word and went to find her son's new domain. Decorated in bright and cheerful yellow and white, the whole large area represented a small boy's heaven. The bed itself was designed to look like a long, low racing car, while the smooth-piled carpet had a pattern of roads and highways similar to the play-mats in use at nursery school.

One wall was devoted to open shelving filled with a selection of toys most children would go for. Nothing cheap, Lian noted, picking up an all-metal dumper truck she had once priced in a store and hastily put down again. Only the best for Bryn Thornley's son.

Far too much at one time, of course. Jonathan was going to be spoiled for choice. She wasn't sure how she felt about such munificence. It couldn't be good for character building to be suddenly given everything this way. The last thing she wanted was for him to become spoiled by over-indulgence.

Something she needed to sort out with Bryn at the earliest opportunity, she decided. Control of her son was not to be relinquished.

Most of the unpacking had been done by the time Bryn put in an appearance. There hadn't, Lian was bound to acknowledge, been all that much to unpack. She was arranging her scanty supply of new toiletries in the bathroom when he arrived. He came to the open door, leaning a shoulder against the jamb with a casual air that somehow irked her.

'I took Jonathan along to his room,' he said. 'He seems pleased with it. How are you doing?'

'I've finished,' she acknowledged. 'All except for Jonathan's things, that is. Most of his older toys can be thrown away. He's hardly going to need them.'

'He must have favourites,' came the level reply. 'Supposing you let him decide for himself.'

He was right, Lian knew, but knowing it didn't help her to accept it. 'He'll be too taken up with all his new things to miss the old,' she returned shortly. 'Why clutter up the place for the sake of it?'

'There's plenty of room.' His voice was unexpectedly tolerant. 'Children and clutter go hand in glove.'

'How would you know?' she demanded. 'You never had one before.'

'Instinct—plus memory. I was a small boy once myself.'

'And that makes you an expert?'

'No, but neither does it make me an incompetent. I'm not trying to buy his affection, just making up for lost time.' The tolerance was beginning to show cracks. 'You have to learn to share him, Lian.'

Part of the price she had to pay; he hadn't actually said the words, but it was what he meant. Rather than expend her energies on a relatively minor matter, she would do better to marshal her reserves against a time when more important issues arose, she reflected. Bryn couldn't expect to take over piecemeal.

'What kind of thing should I wear for this dinner out?' she asked expressionlessly.

If the change of tack in any way disconcerted him, he didn't show it. 'Whatever you like. The Falcon isn't all that formal.' He moved aside to allow her passage back into the bedroom, putting out a hand as she passed him and drawing her round to look at him. The grey eyes were veiled. 'It's going to take time,' he said. 'Let's not make Jonathan the bone of contention between us.'

She was silent, gazing at him with darkened eyes and suddenly increased pulse-rate. She was conscious of the tensile strength in the fingers curled about her elbow, of the hardness of muscle beneath the thin silk of his shirt— of the long-suppressed memories stirring to life again. She wanted him to kiss her, she realised. Wanted it so badly she could feel herself trembling inside.

He made no attempt to comply with her unspoken plea. 'I'll go and take a shower,' he said.

Alone again in the golden evening glow of the bedroom, Lian sank to a seat on the bed-edge and acknowledged the hollow truth. Bryn not only didn't love her, he didn't even want her. Not with any overriding ardour, at any rate. He would perform his husbandly duties because his masculinity demanded it, but in his own time and at his own choosing. That was the message received. They were as far apart as any two people could be.

CHAPTER FIVE

THE Falcon turned out to be a very much up-market hostelry set right on the banks of Windermere itself. Seated at a window table looking across the expanse of shimmering water to the heights of Sca Fell and Langdale Pikes, Lian was moved to comment on the tranquillity of the scene.

'It wouldn't have looked quite the same earlier,' Bryn returned. 'The day trippers turn up in hordes this time of year. There can be as many as two thousand boats on the lake on a fine day. Did you decide what you wanted to eat?'

'I'll have what you're having,' she said, unable to come to any hard and fast decision. 'Small portions, please. I'm not really all that hungry.'

Bryn signalled the hovering waiter and ordered white-bait followed by noisettes of lamb, then took the champagne bottle from its bucket to refill both their glasses. They'd been driven here in the Mercedes by the housekeeper's husband, who combined the duties of occasional chauffeur and general factotum, and were to be picked up again at ten o'clock. Between then and now stretched two hours of conversational no man's land, with the ever-intruding thought of the night to come twisting Lian's stomach muscles.

Enthusiastic or not, Bryn was unlikely to respond to a suggestion that they forgo the ritual. He had his male pride to consider. The only way she was going to be able to go through with it was by drinking to forget. It seemed fitting enough, considering that was how the whole thing had begun. Her head felt a little light already.

It was impossible to be unaware of how devastating he looked in the dark beige suit that sat on his frame the way only the very best tailoring could. Certainly she wasn't the only female in the room who'd noted that fact. He'd been greeted a couple of times by people seated at other tables, and was obviously known to the staff who addressed him by name. As a Thornley, she would probably be expected to play a part in local society. Not a prospect she viewed with any great enthusiasm, but she would do whatever was required of her.

She was wearing her only really good dress in a navy-blue lightweight jersey, once again picked up at a 'nearly new' sale a few months back. With her hair taken up and her new make-up adorning her face, she felt reasonably confident in her appearance. There would have to be additions to her wardrobe, of course, once it was realised just how limited it was, but she had no qualms about that. Fiona dressed beautifully. Bryn would expect no less of her.

'Does your sister have a job of any kind?' she asked, for something to say. 'She doesn't strike me as the type who'd be content to sit around painting her nails all day.'

'She isn't,' he agreed. 'She and a friend run an antiques business in Kendal. Very profitably too. She'd be delighted to show you round if you're interested. Do you drive, by the way?'

'I hold a licence,' Lian admitted, 'but it's been a long time since I last sat behind a wheel.'

'Now's the time to start again. I'll see about getting you a car of your own. Any particular preference?'

She shook her head, feeling suddenly heartened. A car of her own would return some measure of independence. 'Thank you,' she said on a formal note, and saw his mouth take on the familiar slant.

'You're welcome.' There was a pause, a change of tone. 'You might like to know that I've put Jonathan down for a place at Cheddows. That's the prep school I attended myself. He'll be starting right after Christmas.'

'Not boarding?' Lian queried swiftly.

'No, it's only a few miles from here. He can attend on a daily basis. I don't like the idea of sending children away as young as that either. Time enough when he's eleven or twelve.'

Seven more years. Lian couldn't visualise that far ahead. Jonathan was going to be gaining so much from this change in circumstances. Saying goodnight to him earlier, she had been both surprised and a bit disconcerted to realise how quickly he was adjusting to his new lifestyle. He hadn't even shown any adverse reaction to the news that she would be going out for the evening. He was a Thornley in name now as well as fact, and it showed.

The evening took on a rather more relaxed atmosphere as it progressed. Whether due wholly to the champagne, Lian couldn't be sure, but it certainly helped. By the time they were ready to leave, she was feeling no pain. She even found it possible to view the rest of the night without falling apart. Bryn would make love to her, and she would respond, and if it meant nothing very soul-shattering to either of them it was just too bad. There was more to marriage than lovemaking, anyway. Far, far more.

Banks had them back at the house by half-past ten. Even so, both Mrs Thornley and Fiona appeared to have already retired. Lian had sobered by the time they reached their bedroom. She numbly shook her head when

Bryn asked if she wanted first turn in the bathroom. There was always the hope that he might fall asleep while waiting for her to emerge.

The memory of that earlier desire to have him kiss her had been thrust to the back of her mind where it could do the least harm. The way she felt right now, she couldn't bear for him to so much as touch her!

He was wearing black silk pyjamas under a matching robe when he did come out. Lian seized the simple cotton nightdress and wrap she had laid ready, and closed the door between them with her heart thudding painfully against her ribcage, only just resisting the urge to turn the key in the lock.

She took as long as she reasonably could in preparing for bed, but eventually there had to come a time when she could delay the moment no longer. Framed within the cloud of well-brushed chestnut hair, her face in the mirror looked pale without make-up—almost peaky, in fact. The nightdress had narrow straps which tied on each shoulder and left a great deal too much flesh exposed. She donned the wrap and belted it about her waist before nerving herself to open the door again.

Bryn was lying in bed looking at a magazine, the covers draped lightly across his hips. He had removed the robe and his chest was bare, the tight whorls of his body hair evoking an emotion she couldn't deny. Her breasts tingled to the imagined stimulus, her nipples peaking of their own accord beneath the thin cotton. Every detail of that long ago night was fresh in her mind, rousing her despite herself. She couldn't bring herself to move but simply stood there gazing at him.

'You look like a schoolgirl,' he said softly. 'All scrubbed and shining.' He held out a hand. 'Come on over here.'

She went on nerveless limbs to take the hand and allow herself to be drawn down to him. His lips were cool and quite gentle at first, teasing rather than forceful. She let herself drift in the sensation, not thinking anything, just feeling.

It took the touch of his lips at her throat to waken her from the dream state. Her wrap was unfastened, his hand beginning a slow and subtle exploration of her slender curves. Like last time, yet not like last time, because the emotions he was arousing in her now went far beyond those younger limitations. It had been so long, so very, very long since she had known this kind of enthralment. The reticence of these past hours was totally forgotten in the rising heat engendered by his caresses.

The tie-straps of her nightdress gave easily, allowing him to draw the material away from her upper body. The hand at her breast was almost delicate in its stroking, circling motion. She gasped when he lowered his head to take her tingling nipple between his lips, back arching to the exquisite sensation. She could hear the pulsing of his heartbeats, smell the emotive male scent of his body, feel the vibrant manhood pressuring her thighs apart. She'd been wrong about one thing: Bryn wanted her all right. No man could conjure such swift and certain physiological evidence by will alone.

It was only when he eventually slid the nightdress the whole way down her body and tossed it away that she realised he was already fully naked himself. She spread her limbs instinctively to receive him, little incoherent moans escaping her lips as they joined and became one. Then he was moving and she was following, losing all sense of time and place in the wild hunger that filled her. They were together again and nothing else mattered. Together!

It was some time before he stirred after that final and mind-searing implosion. Even then he made no attempt to turn away from her, propping himself on an elbow to study her shape by the soft glow of the bedside lamp with open and warming appreciation.

'The way I remember you,' he murmured. 'Smooth and firm and lovely!' He splayed the fingers of one hand across the fluttering skin of her abdomen, smiling at the fresh leap of expression in her eyes. 'And responsive. I remember that too. I never thought to see you again, Lian.'

'You wouldn't have done,' she said softly, 'if it hadn't been for Jonathan. I'd probably have been married to someone else by now.'

'His loss, my gain.' He put his lips to her temple where the hair clung damply, kissing the pulse which beat just below the skin. 'We'll just have to make up for the missing years the best way we can.'

He was talking about Jonathan, of course, Lian told herself. It was going to take time to form the kind of relationship he would want with his son. Mostly it depended on how much effort he was prepared to put into the development.

His lips had reached the point of her jaw. She felt her senses stir once more as he ran the tip of his tongue over the tender skin behind her earlobe. Her hands lifted flat against his chest, fingers spreading through the wiry hair to curl in involuntary spasm as the lightly probing tongue found another erogenous zone. His body was signalling renewal, eliciting her own tremoring revitalisation. She could never, came the misty thought, have enough of this!

*   *   *

By the end of the week, Jonathan might never have lived anywhere else but at Revedon. For him, every day was a delight. The staff, without exception, were totally won over by the young addition to the family. Mrs Banks in particular revealed a side to her nature that Lian wouldn't have suspected on first acquaintance.

'He's a charmer,' confirmed Bryn in some amusement. 'He can twist the lot of us round his little finger without even trying!'

'He's had too much to occupy his mind to get into any mischief yet,' Lian warned, 'but that doesn't mean he's incapable of it. He was something of a ringleader in nursery school.'

The amusement increased. 'That's not bad going at four and a half. He might make Prime Minister yet!'

The two of them were on their way into Kendal to choose the car he had promised her. Jonathan having been left in the charge of his grandmother for the morning, there was no one around to break the pause after that last remark. Not an uncomfortable silence, Lian reflected, squinting against the sun to bring a distant black speck into sharper focus, more of a companionable one.

'Is that an eagle hovering over there?' she asked. 'It looks big enough.'

'Probably nearer than you think, and a hawk or kestrel,' Bryn returned. 'Eagles don't normally hunt outside their own territory.'

Wearing a casual cotton shirt and light trousers, he looked very much the way he had that first morning. Not even a full fortnight ago until tomorrow, Lian realised. So much had happened since then, she could scarcely believe it.

Had anyone told her only last week that she would feel as good as she did right now, she wouldn't have believed that either. But then, that was before the wedding night which Bryn had made so memorable. Last night too, if it came to that. If love was missing it didn't show; she couldn't even say she felt the lack all that deeply herself. They were attuned in other ways, and that counted for a lot.

'You'll not be away longer than a few days next week, will you?' she asked now on a casual note.

His shrug was non-committal. 'Depends what crops up. I may have to spend some extra time with the American contingent.' He slanted a quizzical glance. 'Shall you miss me?'

'Of course,' she responded, equally lightly. 'I'm going to be doing some exploring while you're gone. There are so many lovely places to visit.'

'True enough. A pity I can't do it with you.' He sounded genuinely regretful. 'Maybe I should cut loose and run the estate instead.'

'And put Duncan out of a job?' she said, taking the suggestion no more seriously than she was sure he intended it to be taken.

'There is that.' He sent another brief glance her way. 'What do you think of him?'

Lian had met the estate controller on the Thursday morning when he had come to the house to see Bryn. In his early forties, and ruggedly attractive, he had struck her favourably enough. She said as much now.

'He's good at his job,' he agreed. 'My father took him on not long before he died. There's just something about the man I don't——' He broke off, shaking his head dismissively. 'No matter.'

They reached the town to find it busy with both motorised and pedestrian traffic. Bryn drove straight to a small but obviously exclusive showroom, and invited Lian to take her pick from the three vehicles presented by the salesman on hearing what was required.

Never an expert when it came to naming different makes and models, she was capable of recognising the Mercedes emblem when she saw it. The sporty shape and deep red gloss of the 450 SL convertible took her eye immediately. A car anyone would love to own, she admitted, trying to retain a certain nonchalance in front of the salesman. Jonathan would be over the moon to ride in it!

With insurance fixed, and arrangements made to have the car delivered to Revedon the following morning, there still remained a couple of hours till lunchtime. Asked what she would like to do next, Lian plumped for paying Fiona a visit at the shop. Bryn seemed oddly reticent, but as he didn't refuse she could only conclude she was imagining things.

Built of the grey limestone which characterised the town, the Copper Kettle was one of a small parade of shops devoted to the quality end of the market. Fiona was busy arranging one of the bow-fronted windows to show a single superb Chippendale chair against a back-cloth of draped velvet. She looked a little taken aback when Lian tapped on the glass to attract her attention, but only for a moment, then she smiled and indicated the door.

A young woman Lian took to be her sister-in-law's partner came through from the rear premises in answer to the chime of a bell as they entered. She was tall and willowy in an Italian-knit suit of finest cream cotton, her blonde hair drawn back into a smooth chignon. Only the most perfect of bone-structures could take that severity of style, conceded Lian admiringly.

The lack of warmth in the blue eyes was the only marring factor. They were like chips of ice. Bryn was the first to speak, voice as expressionless as only he could make it.

'Christine, I'd like you to meet my wife.'

The nod was perfunctory, the greeting even more so. 'Hello.'

Lian returned the nod, but summoned a smile to go with it. 'Hello. If you're busy right now I can always come back another time.'

'Now is fine,' said Fiona, coming out of the window. 'Did you find the right car?'

'Couldn't be better!' Lian did her best to sound as enthusiastic as she had felt about it earlier, only it was somehow difficult with Madam Frost standing there listening. 'A convertible. All I'm going to need is for this weather to keep up so I can have the top down. I'll have to take a few test runs around the grounds before I venture out on the roads with it, though. I haven't driven for ages.'

She was talking too much, she knew, but it was better than staying silent. The atmosphere was oppressive. 'Do you mind if I take a look around the shop?' she tagged on, by way of changing the subject. 'You have some lovely pieces.'

'You're knowledgeable about antiques?' queried Christine on a sceptical note.

'Not in the same way you two obviously are,' Lian returned evenly, 'but I can tell the difference between quality and tat.'

'Let me show you the new pieces we're pricing up in the back,' offered Fiona without haste. She glanced at her brother. 'Bryn?'

He shook his head without looking up from the Tunbridgeware cribbage board he was appraising. 'I'll wait out here. This is a Barton, isn't it?'

It was Christine who answered. 'Yes, it is. Are you interested?'

She was moving to join him as Lian followed Fiona. The two of them made a striking couple, she was bound to admit—the one so dark, the other so fair. There was something in the way Bryn had looked at the woman that elicited a certain misgiving. Coupled with that slight hesitation over coming here to the shop at all, and Christine's cool reception, it began to look as if there might have been an attachment of some kind between them before she appeared on the scene.

The only sure way of finding out was to ask Fiona. She put the question in as forthright a manner as she could manage, to have the suspicion confirmed by the other's discomfiture.

'It wasn't a long-term thing,' she asserted. 'There was nothing serious between them. Not on Bryn's part, anyway.'

Lian said softly. 'Did he tell you that?'

'Well, no, not in so many words, but I do happen to know him pretty well.' Fiona gave her an appraising glance. 'It's obviously over now, so does it really matter?'

It wasn't over for Christine, Lian reflected. Not from the way she was acting. She could even find a certain sympathy for her. The discovery that Bryn was not only to be married but had a child into the bargain was hardly likely to have delighted her. Small wonder that he hadn't been keen to come and face her.

By tacit consent the subject was dropped. Lian conjured an interest in the items Fiona was showing her, but her heart wasn't in it. While she realised Bryn had been no monk, it was something else again to be confronted with one of his ex-girlfriends—especially when she looked the way Christine looked. He must have compared the two of them: she in the same green linen suit she had worn that first day, the other so elegantly and expensively clad. It was impossible not to feel disadvantaged.

They were still talking when she and Fiona returned to the shop floor—a conversation broken off apparently in mid-sentence as Bryn moved abruptly away.

'I'm taking the cribbage board,' he said to his sister. 'Christine has the cheque.' Grey eyes met green, the former revealing no hint of his thoughts. 'Nothing you fancied yourself?'

Lian shook her head, not trusting her voice.

'Then we'd better be getting back. I promised Jonathan a swimming lesson this afternoon.'

Christine had disappeared into the rear, leaving Fiona to make the farewells. Bryn started the car and headed for home in silence. Stealing the occasional glance at the firm profile, Lian was tempted to ask what was wrong, just to see what his answer would be, but something inside her resisted the urge. If his mood was related in any way at all to the lovely Christine, she didn't want to know.

They found Jonathan with Banks in the garage courtyard. He'd been helping wash the cars, he informed them importantly.

'Afraid he got a bit wet,' apologised the chauffeur. 'I was just about to take him in to get changed.'

'A 'bit' was an understatement, thought Lian, viewing the sodden shorts and sandals. Not that it would do him any harm on a warm day like this. Back on even keel again, Bryn swung the small figure up on to his shoulders, ignoring the moisture soaking into his shirt. Jonathan shrieked with excitement and clutched at his hair as he jogged into the house.

'Such a noise!' exclaimed Mrs Thornley, coming to the sitting-room door to see what was happening, but there was an indulgent note in her voice as she regarded the two male Thornleys. 'How on earth did you manage to get in that state, young man?'

'I'd say hose-pipe, at a guess,' supplied her son in passing. He looked back at Lian to add, 'I'll see to him. You stay and talk to Mother.'

Following the older woman back into the room with some reluctance, Lian took a seat and waited for her to set the ball rolling. Circumstances made it difficult to feel at ease with her mother-in-law; she couldn't imagine they would ever achieve any real closeness. The marriage was accepted because of Jonathan, no other reason. Honour had been satisfied.

'I assume you found a car,' was the opening remark. 'I can't understand why Bryn didn't have one or two nice saloons brought out for you to look at right here, if you have to have your own. One would think there were quite enough vehicles cluttering up the premises as it is!'

'I suppose he thought it would be simpler if I didn't have to rely on you not needing the Mercedes if I wanted to go anywhere,' Lian replied mildly, wondering what the reaction to the SL was going to be. 'A little independence can only be a good thing.'

'Always providing you don't abuse it.'

'I shan't do that.' Lian waited a moment before adding impulsively, 'I know how you must feel about me, Mrs Thornley. I'd probably feel the same if I had to face the same situation with Jonathan in years to come. To be honest, if I'd known what was going to come of that visit I made a couple of weeks ago, I don't think I'd have gone through with it. I'm out of my depth here.'

There was no smile on the other face, just the same inflexible regard. 'Time will tell,' she said. 'My son did his duty by you; I expect you to do yours by him. The Thornley name has some standing in this part of the world.'

'I'm sure it does.' Lian relinquished the attempt to bridge the gap. There might eventually come a time when her mother-in-law learned to trust her, but that time wasn't yet. For the present she had to be content in the knowledge that Jonathan at least was accepted.

Father and son came back downstairs together. They were both of them changed into fresh clothing, and seemed to be getting on like a house on fire—which left Lian feeling even more out of things. She'd had Jonathan to herself for too long to find the sharing easy. Another battle she had to fight.

The promised swimming lesson was scheduled for mid-afternoon, after lunch had had time to settle. Lian had taken a brief look at the pool, which was enclosed within glass walls, and heated. At Bryn's suggestion, she joined the pair of them, watching with stifled jealousy as he overcame Jonathan's reservations about deep water and taught him first how to float on top of it. She should have taken him to one of the municipal pools herself before this, she knew, but they were always so crowded, and joining clubs cost too much in subscriptions.

It had been years since she had last been in the water herself. Paddling in the sea on one of their infrequent trips to the coast hardly counted. Two lengths of the pool was all she could manage. Even then, she was puffing like a grampus when she finished.

'I'm badly out of condition,' she admitted wryly, hanging on to the side rail close by where Bryn was holding Jonathan up by the chin while he practised kicking his legs in the prescribed manner. 'I didn't realise just how much!'

'A few lengths every morning, and you'll soon be on top of it,' he returned. 'You'll be able to continue the lessons while I'm away.' To his son he added encouragingly, 'We'll have you swimming Windermere next month!'

Allowing his legs to sink in perfect trust of the man holding him, Jonathan looked up with a trace of anxiety in his eyes. 'Are you going away for long?'

Bryn shook his head. 'No longer than I can help.'

'Why?'

'Why am I going?' The smile was accompanied by a shrug. 'I often ask myself the same question. Things run perfectly well without me.'

'I doubt it.' Lian's tone had a dry quality she couldn't fully eradicate. 'Daddy has to work, Jonathan, in order to feed and clothe us all.'

She had used the title deliberately, partly for her son's benefit, partly to underline the fact in her own mind. Meeting Bryn's glance, she felt warmth run under her skin. He was perfectly well aware of her feelings, and, from his expression, more than a little intolerant of them.

But then, he couldn't be expected to understand, could he? So far as he was concerned, she had gained far more than she had lost.

If anything, she supposed he was the main loser. He not only had a son he hadn't bargained for, but his bachelor freedom of choice was a thing of the past. At least, she hoped it was. Since meeting Christine this morning she couldn't be a hundred per cent sure. Whatever it was that had been between them, it still existed. The question was whether he could bring himself to give up all such interests in favour of a wife he didn't love but felt obligated towards. She didn't want his attentions on any kind of duty footing, regardless of how well he performed the function.

'Speaking of clothes,' he said now on a level note, 'you might like to start using the account I've opened for you. They'll need a sample signature at the bank before you write any cheques, but it's only a formality. I think you'll find the allowance generous enough.'

'I'm sure I shall.' They were like two strangers again, Lian thought painfully, and mostly due to her own lack of trust. She had to forget about Christine. Otherwise it was no good going on at all. She forced a smile, a lighter note. 'I'll try not to use it all at once!'

'I'm going to get dressed and play with Sam,' announced Jonathan, losing interest in swimming for the moment.

'I'll come and help you,' said Lian, but he firmly rejected the offer.

'I can dress myself!'

Bryn hoisted him up the ladder, putting out a hand to stop Lian from following him as he scampered off to the changing cubicles. 'He'll manage. He might finish up a bit damp again, but he'll soon dry off.'

Subsiding back into the water, she made an effort to see his point of view. Jonathan had been dressing himself for almost a year now. Towelling himself down first certainly wasn't beyond his powers.

'You're quite right,' she said generously. 'I'm being too much of the mother hen.'

'A very fetching one.' His tone had altered, the line of his mouth relaxing. 'You have the figure for a bikini. Too few do.'

He had moved in front of her as she stood with arms stretched along the rail at her back, the water at this level lapping about his waistline. Droplets glistened in his chest hair, turning it silver in places. In close-up, and wet, his shoulders looked massive. Lian had an urge to run her fingers along the lines of muscle and feel that contained power.

'You're crowding me,' she whispered as he moved in closer to pin her against the side.

'I know,' he said, and kissed her, sliding his hands along her arms to hold her in position. 'I've been wanting to do this since you got into the damned pool,' he growled in her ear.

Pulse hammering like crazy, she made a valiant attempt to push him away. 'Jonathan will see us!'

'He was too intent on getting out to bother coming back,' came the unmoved response. 'My kissing you isn't going to cause him any traumas anyway.'

'How can you be sure?' Lian demanded weakly as his lips moved down the side of her throat to her shoulder. 'It's not unknown.'

The sound of a door closing was all the answer Bryn obviously deemed necessary. Dry or not, Jonathan had gone to find his beloved Sam. He wouldn't be back.

The removal of her bra top drew a faint protest from her all the same. Not that it made any difference. Cupping both breasts, he bent to kiss each aching nipple, running his tongue around the aureole in a caress that roused her to fever pitch. Only when he slid his hands around her back to ease the band of her briefs away from her skin did she make any further objection. 'Bryn, no!'

'Bryn, yes,' he said softly. 'I want you, Lian. Now— this minute!'

She wanted him too, only not here. She was incapable of shutting her mind to everything else the way he apparently could. 'Someone might come!'

'Only if they have the chance.' He straightened away from her, irony in the line of his mouth as he studied her flushed face. 'Making love in the water is a whole new experience. You might have enjoyed it.'

Meaning he'd done it before with someone else, she surmised, and felt the ache set in deep down. Perhaps he'd even brought Christine here some time.

'I'm sorry if you're already bored enough to need that kind of diversion,' she said stiffly, and saw his expression undergo a swift and indefinable change.

'I didn't say that.'

She was shivering a little despite the warmth of the water. 'You implied it.'

'Then *I'm* sorry. It certainly wasn't intended that way.' He moved abruptly away to hoist himself out of the pool. 'We'll call it a day, shall we? It's about time for tea, in any case.'

Lian watched him stride off in the direction of the changing cubicles, her heart heavy as lead. What rapport they had managed to attain was degenerating fast, and it was mostly her own fault. It took more than a few kisses to keep a man like Bryn Thornley satisfied.

CHAPTER SIX

BYRN left for Manchester first thing Monday morning. He would be spending the day there, then travelling down to London on the Tuesday. He would, he said, telephone once he knew what his commitments for the week to come were likely to be.

Seeing him off, Lian knew despondency. She wasn't yet accustomed enough to living at Revedon to feel any sense of belonging, and her mother-in-law showed little sign yet of cordiality. It was going to take time and patience to convince her that Bryn hadn't made such a bad bargain.

Whether Bryn himself was of that opinion was open to question. Although he had made no further reference to Friday's little conflict at the pool, there had been a certain reserve in his manner, as if he were deliberately holding back. Lian would have liked to be able to discuss the matter frankly and openly, but shrank from being the one to broach it. How could he be expected to understand that her reticence had been as much a product of self-doubt as fear of being caught in the act?

Fiona came out from the house as she turned to go back in.

'Sorry to dash off,' the other apologised, 'but I'm on my own this morning. Christine's going to be attending auctions most of the week.'

'Does she do all the buying?' asked Lian.

'No, but we can't both be out together, and it's her turn to do the rounds. Hopefully she'll pick up some good pieces.' A hand was lifted in brief farewell. 'See you tonight.'

A whole day to fill before then, thought Lian, carefully blanking her mind to the disturbing suspicion which had flashed across it. Hardly a difficult task, considering.

The SL had been delivered as promised on the Saturday morning, and Bryn had accompanied her on a drive around the district while she got used to the feel of the controls. After ten minutes he had pronounced her perfectly competent to go it alone, which was reassuring. She intended taking it for a run this afternoon, along with Jonathan *and* Sam, as the former was reluctant to be parted from his pal for longer than absolutely necessary. They could go up round Windermere and give the animal some exercise in new surroundings.

There was no sign of her mother-in-law when she went back indoors. Hillary, the maid, who was clearing the breakfast things, told her the mistress often spent weekday mornings in her own room writing letters and such. Left to her own devices, and with the estate not open to the public on Mondays, it would be a good time to do a little exploring outside of the private sector of the grounds, Lian decided. If she was ever going to call this place home, she had to become familiar with the whole of it.

Wearing comfortable old jeans and short-sleeved shirt, she set out via the side-yard with Jonathan and Sam in tow. Banks had the SL out and was giving it a loving extra polish. He'd always fancied a sports car for his own use, he confided when Lian thanked him for the care and attention he was lavishing on the car, only Mrs Banks didn't hold with such frivolities.

Neither did Mrs Thornley, reflected Lian drily. Her comments had been very much to the point. Not that Bryn had seemed unduly perturbed. He'd even backed her driving ability.

She was going to miss him, she acknowledged. No matter what the circumstances, his presence was preferable to his absence. The thought of several days, perhaps a whole week, without him was depressing. By the time he returned, she wanted to be in the right frame of mind to meet him on equal terms. Marriage needed working at if it was going to be any good at all. Sexually, she was still a novice, but she could learn. She would do whatever was required to keep him reasonably content. That much she owed him.

They visited the farm first. Samson, Lian was pleased to find, paid no more than a passing attention to the other animals. He even allowed a couple of hens to peck their way across the yard right under his nose without turning a hair.

Mr Thornley had made a habit of bringing the dog over several times a week from the time when he was just a puppy to get him used to being with other livestock, Dorothy Baxter confirmed. She invited Lian into her comfortable and roomy kitchen for coffee while her husband kept boy and dog occupied in the yard.

'I can't imagine ever living anywhere else but at Revedon,' she said when Lian asked her how she liked being a tenant rather than an owner. 'The Thornleys have always been good people to work for. This way we can have the life we like without the worry.' She added with enthusiasm, 'Things have been better still since the house was reopened to the public. I'm thoroughly enjoying taking parties round again. It's a pity Mr Thornley had to wait for his father to pass on before he could do anything about restoring it properly, but he's made a marvellous job of it.'

'Wonderful,' agreed Lian, privately thinking she would have preferred a home like this one if she'd had a choice at all. Except that she couldn't imagine Bryn in any setting other than Revedon. He belonged.

Over the following hour or so, they managed to cover only a small part of the extensive acreage. The woodland backing the house was deliciously cool and quiet, with narrow pathways meandering through it without apparent purpose or design. There were squirrels in the trees, much to Jonathan's delight, and a preponderance of bird life. Filtering through the leafy branches, the sunlight formed long rays in which a fine smoke seemed to curl.

Beyond the woods lay the southern boundary of the estate. A couple of gardeners were at work trimming the twelve-foot-tall yew hedges on the far side of the perimeter roadway. Recognising the younger of the pair as their friend from the bus that very first morning, Lian gave him a bright 'Hello!', unsurprised to see him somewhat at a loss for a suitable reply. The last time they had met she had been just another visitor, now here she was a member of the family.

'Good morning,' he replied courteously in the end. 'Lost, are you?'

'A bit,' she admitted. 'I suppose if we follow the road it will bring us back to the house eventually.'

'It's some dis——' he began, then broke off as the sound of an engine heralded the approach of some vehicle. 'Here comes Mr Fleming,' he said. 'He'll take you back.'

Lian moved to the side of the road again as the Land Rover hove into view around the far bend. They were going to need a lift if they were to make lunch. She summoned a smile for the man she had met only twice up to now as he brought the car to a halt in front of her.

'Hello there,' he said easily. 'Looking for a lift?'

'I think we have to be,' she agreed. 'I hadn't realised how far we'd come.'

'Climb aboard,' he invited. 'I'll have you back in a jiffy.'

She helped Jonathan into the back first, holding the door for Samson to join him. Sliding into the front passenger seat, she said tentatively, 'I hope we're not taking you out of your way.'

'Makes no difference if you are. It's only going to take five minutes.' He glanced sideways at her, square-jawed face registering a frank appraisal. 'What do you think of the place so far?'

'It's very beautiful.' Lian cudgelled her brains for some less trite comment, but could only come up with, 'And extremely well kept.'

'We do our best. More easily, I might add, since Bryn took over. I spent twelve months trying to persuade his father to do what he's done, but the old man would never spend a pound where a penny would do. I had my work cut out just keeping the place from going to rack and ruin completely. The previous estate manager hadn't given it too much of his time and effort, and that's a fact!'

'What made you take on the job if things were that bad?' asked Lian curiously.

'The challenge, I suppose,' he admitted. 'Plus the locality. I'm from the south. I wanted a complete change of environment after losing my wife.' He caught her reaction, and shook his head, lips twisting. 'Wrong sense. She went off with another man.'

'I'm sorry.' Lian scarcely knew what else to say.

'Oh, I got over it. She was a bitch anyway.' He gave her a brief smile. 'If you'll excuse the expression.'

Lian made no reply. He had told her far more than she had wanted to know—far more than he should have been prepared to impart to an almost complete stranger. She couldn't imagine Bryn being as free with his private affairs in any circumstances. Having said that, one had to feel a certain sympathy for the man. The hurt had obviously gone deep enough to turn him bitter. Losing a partner that way had to be a traumatic experience.

'You've created quite a stir in the area yourself,' he commented frankly. 'There's been many a hope dashed by this marriage of Bryn's.'

'He's my daddy,' chimed in Jonathan from the rear. 'Did you know?'

The eyes briefly turned Lian's way held a meaningful glint. 'Nobody could doubt it, son.'

'I'm not *your* son,' came the logical response. 'Only Daddy's. He was lost for a long time, but we found him again, didn't we, Mummy?'

'Yes, we did.' Lian could feel her cheeks burning. 'Don't let Sam chew the seat, Jonathan.'

'Tenacity pays off in the end.' Duncan Fleming's tone was openly admiring. 'You certainly won out this time!'

The house was in sight, to Lian's relief. She should tell him to mind his own damned business, she knew, but the words wouldn't come. He was only voicing what everyone else was probably thinking. Who would believe she hadn't had her own interests at heart in coming to Revedon?

If the truth were only known, she sometimes had doubts herself. Her feelings on first seeing that photograph of Bryn had been so mixed; wasn't it just possible that she had made Jonathan's educational needs an excuse rather than the prime motive? That night with Bryn had left more than one kind of imprint; it had spoiled her for lesser men. There had been a couple of occasions over the years when she could have formed a worthwhile relationship, but she hadn't wanted to know.

Not that it mattered what her motivation had been, she supposed. She was Bryn's wife, for better or for worse. What she had to do now was concentrate on making the marriage work out regardless.

Duncan drew the Land Rover to a showy halt outside the double gates leading through to the side-yard, scattering gravel in the process. He leapt out before Lian could gather herself together, and came round to open the door for her with a mock bow. 'Home, your ladyship!'

Short of being downright rude, she could scarcely ignore the hand he held out to her. She took it reluctantly, forcing a laugh to lighten the moment. 'Thank you, Duncan!'

Jonathan gave vent to a sudden joyful shout and almost fell from the car in his haste to reach the man who had appeared in the opened gateway. Bryn swung him up in ready arms, the smile on his face not reaching the grey eyes as they regarded the couple still standing by the Land Rover.

'Having fun?' he asked.

Too astonished to see him again so soon after his departure to make any immediate move towards him, Lian said blankly, 'Did you forget something?'

'A rather vital file,' he returned. 'I was halfway to Manchester before I realised it. A nuisance, but my own fault. I should have double checked my briefcase before I left.'

'What about your board meeting?'

'They'll have to wait for me, won't they?' He put Jonathan down again, resting a light hand on the boy's head. 'I gather you got yourselves lost?'

'I picked them up over by the south boundary,' said Duncan before Lian could answer for herself. 'I'll be getting back now they're home safe and sound.' He gave Lian a smiling salute. 'At your service any time, ma'am!'

Bryn watched the other man turn the Land Rover in a tight circle and drive off, then looked back at Lian expressionlessly. 'I phoned through and put the board meeting back to three o'clock, so I'll be staying for lunch.'

'Oh, good.' It sounded totally inadequate, but there was little else to say. 'I suppose we should let Mrs Banks know.'

'I already told her,' he said. 'I was coming to look for you, but I see I needn't have bothered.'

'We walked a long way through the wood,' Jonathan told him, 'Miles and miles!'

Looking down at the diminutive figure in his grubby shorts and shirt, Bryn's face softened a little. 'That's a lot of exercise. It might be a good idea to go and have a quiet play upstairs until it's time to get ready for lunch.'

'Will you come too?' asked Jonathan, apparently not averse to the idea.

'Not right now,' came the firm reply. 'I want to talk to your mother. You can take Sam instead.'

The small face lit up. To have the dog with him in his room was a new and infinitely desirable innovation.

Calling the animal, he set off at a run for the house before any minds could be changed.

'Mrs Banks is going to be delighted to find dog hairs all over his carpet,' Lian commented, following with Bryn at a more sedate pace.

'Vacuum cleaners were invented some time ago,' he responded. He paused before adding curtly. 'I don't want you getting too friendly with Fleming.'

She glanced at him in some disconcertion, taking in the set of his jaw. 'Why?'

'Because I say so. Isn't that enough?'

Her jaw took on a jut of its own. She might not care overmuch for the estate manager, but this was something else. 'I'm afraid it isn't. I'm likely to be running into him pretty often. What am I supposed to do, pretend he doesn't exist?'

'Just don't encourage familiarities. He's likely to take advantage.'

'I'm not sure what that's supposed to mean.'

They had almost reached the door. Bryn paused to look down at her with an uncompromising expression. 'You hardly need it spelling out for you.'

'I need a better reason than you've just given me,' she retorted, bridling at his tone. 'I may be new to this kind of lifestyle, Bryn, but I'm not a puppet to dance to whatever tune you happen to call. Duncan gave me...us a lift back to the house after we got a bit off track, that's all. He took no liberties.' She deliberately closed her mind to the memory of his presumptuous remarks. Words never hurt anyone. 'I don't care for being told what to do as if I weren't capable of acting on my own initiative!'

'Finished?' he asked stonily.

She was too incensed to heed any danger signals. A
marriage licence gave him no right to dictate her actions.
Not in this day and age. 'No, I'm not finished!'

'I am,' he said, and carried on into the house, leaving
her standing there looking after him like a dummy.

Self-righteous anger got her moving again. She caught
him up at the foot of the stairs, eyes flashing green fire
as she faced him across the balustrade.

'Who is it you really don't trust, Bryn?' she demanded.
'Duncan, or me?'

He observed her dispassionately, one hand resting on
the newel post. 'I'm not prepared to carry on an
argument with you,' he said. 'You know my views. All
you have to do is respect them.'

'Don't you mean *obey*?'

'If you want to see it that way. I'm going to fetch the
file I came back for. I'd suggest you change out of those
jeans before lunch.'

Lian had intended to do that anyway, but wasn't about
to say so. The intimation that her sense of propriety
couldn't be relied on was hurtful. She'd given him no
call to doubt her in any way, she was sure.

He carried on up the stairs when she stayed silent.
Gazing after the retreating back, she could only seethe
inwardly and impotently. She'd had glimpses of this
uncompromising aspect when opposed before, but this
was more than a glimpse. The episode had brought home
to her how little she really knew him.

With an hour yet to go until lunchtime, she briefly
contemplated doing a disappearing act just for the hell
of it, then reluctantly accepted that such behaviour was
off limits, if only for Jonathan's sake. The same went
for defying his recommendation and turning up for the

meal still wearing the outfit she had on now. She would be the one to feel discomfited.

Still seething, she went up to the bedroom and took a shower before getting into a blue cotton dress which had seen better days but was wearable. So far she hadn't touched a penny of the allowance Bryn had made her. Right at this moment, she felt like throwing the cheque-book back in his face. It was a wonder he wasn't insisting she had help in choosing the new wardrobe she so badly needed.

She had to nip this whole thing in the bud before it went any further, she told herself with determination. There was no way she intended knuckling under to the heavy-husband treatment, whatever the circumstances. Bryn might have done the honourable thing in marrying her, but that didn't mean he owned her. If she kept Duncan Fleming at a distance at all it would be because she wanted to, not because she was ordered.

The sound of laughter drew her along the corridor to Jonathan's room when she went out. Her hand on the doorknob about to turn it, she paused at the sound of Bryn's voice through the panels. Whatever the two of them were doing together, it was causing her son much hilarity. He sounded bubbling over with sheer high spirits.

What she was feeling was jealousy, pure and simple, Lian conceded wryly, taking her hand off the knob again in reluctance to break in on the scene. Jonathan had found a side to his father not open to herself.

The reason being that he was all Bryn had really wanted in the first place; she was just the price he had needed to pay in order to have that wish granted. The lovemaking meant nothing. The word itself was only a euphemism, anyway, in their particular case. What feelings he had for her had never been more than physical.

She had to find herself something to occupy her mind, she thought, drifting aimlessly downstairs. Fiona had a job; why shouldn't she? Jonathan was hardly going to come to any harm with so many people around to look after him. Mrs Banks would be only too delighted to take charge in her absence.

But doing what? That was the sixty-thousand-dollar question. She had little enough experience to offer an employer. If Fiona hadn't been in partnership with Christine, she might have offered to help out in the shop, but the latter made that idea a definite non-starter.

The mere thought of the beautiful blonde was enough to renew the suspicions she had entertained earlier. It was just a little too coincidental that she should be away from the shop at the very same time that Bryn was to be absent from home. They could have arranged to meet in London. Who was to see them together down there? They had certainly been discussing something of import the other morning.

Mrs Thornley eyed the cheap cotton dress with some obvious disdain when the family gathered for lunch, but refrained from immediate comment. For her son's wife to go around looking like a reject from Oxfam was an insult to their standing. Lian resolved to do some serious shopping the following morning in order not to give her mother-in-law any further cause for complaint. To be able to buy what she wanted without thinking about the cost could scarcely be called an onerous task, whatever the objective.

Bryn seemed to have forgotten their contretemps. On the other hand, Lian was beginning to appreciate just how difficult it was to tell what he *was* thinking and feeling. She wondered if anyone had ever managed to achieve a breakthrough to the inner man. Christine didn't come across as a particularly sensitive type, but then looks could be deceiving. There had almost certainly been more to that relationship than Fiona seemed to believe.

'I'm considering looking for a job of some kind,' she announced without preamble over coffee. 'I can't not do anything.'

Mrs Thornley's eyebrows rose. 'I'd have thought looking after Jonathan was enough to be going on with,' she declared. 'Most mothers would be only too glad to have the time and opportunity.'

Jonathan had been excused coffee in order to join Sam on the terrace for half an hour before his afternoon rest. Apart from the pool, which was hardly deep enough to present any danger, and which he knew not to go near in any case, he was perfectly safe and happy out there, Lian reflected. He didn't need her around every minute of the day—in all probability, it wasn't even good for him to become reliant on her always being there, especially with school just over the horizon.

'He's been used to my being away at least part of the day,' she said. 'I doubt if he'd feel in any way deprived. Fiona works,' she added on a defensive note she hadn't intended to employ.

'Fiona doesn't have a child,' returned her mother-in-law. She appealed to her son. 'Bryn, you surely must have something to say about this...notion?'

'It's rather more than just a notion,' Lian rejoined with asperity before he could make any reply. 'And it would be *my* decision.'

'What exactly did you have in mind?' asked Bryn on a surprisingly mild note. 'It would obviously have to be local. You might find opportunities rather limited.'

She eyed him for a moment in somewhat nonplussed silence. The difference in his reaction to this from the way he had been earlier was confusing. 'I hadn't really got that far,' she admitted. 'I'd have to see what was available.'

'That sounds sensible.' There was just the merest hint of satire in the latter observation. He glanced at his watch. 'I have to go. Why don't you walk me to the car?'

More of an instruction than an invitation, Lian thought, but she rose with him anyway. If he wanted to speak his mind out of his mother's hearing, that was OK with her. Only he wasn't going to find her any more amenable to dogmatism than he had on the previous occasion.

He had left his briefcase ready in the hall. Heading for the outer door, with Lian keeping pace at his side, he said levelly, 'I'm not sure whether you meant all that to be taken seriously, but it's hardly a viable proposition. Kendal is the only place you'd be likely to find anything, and even then with the greatest of difficulty. There must be a fair number of unemployed in the town to start with.'

'Meaning I'd be stealing the bread from needy mouths if I did manage to find a job?' Lian made no effort to restrain the rancour. 'I suppose I have to reconcile myself to boredom, then.'

His shrug signified impatience. 'There's plenty you could find to do if you put your mind to it.'

'Like good works, for instance?' Her laugh was brittle. 'I don't see myself as the Lady of the Manor dispensing soup to the down and outs!'

'Apart from the occasional tramp, you'd have a hard job finding any round here,' came the dry retort. 'Try taking up a hobby. You might turn out to have a talent you didn't even realise. It's happened before.'

They were outside now under a sky swiftly clouding over. Significant of the way things were going down here too, thought Lian with a sudden pang. Bryn must be glad to be leaving.

'I'll think about it,' she said, attempting to make some restoration. 'I just can't accustom myself to having time on my hands, that's all.'

'Understandable.' Bryn was obviously making some effort himself to judge from his tone. 'Why don't you ask Mother if she has any suggestions?'

'She already thinks I should be content with my lot the way it is,' Lian reminded him tartly, forgetting the mollification. 'So far as your mother is concerned, I'm showing the utmost ingratitude all the way through!'

'You both need time to get to know one another,' he returned. 'She's set in her ways, and you're...'

'I'm what?' she demanded as he paused in apparent consideration of the right word. 'Too lacking in the necessary refinements?'

Opening the car door to toss in the briefcase, he said coolly, 'Now you're being ridiculous. If I'd thought that, you wouldn't be standing here at all.'

'I'm standing here,' she declared with intent, 'because you knew darned well you'd never have Jonathan otherwise. I'm not fool enough to believe you'd have married me for any other reason, Bryn. The only emotion we share is a concern for our son's future. For *that*, I'm grateful, nothing else.'

He was very still, the hand resting on the car door white-knuckled. 'If I had the time,' he said in low but far from soft tones, 'I'd show you an emotion you didn't take into account. I don't want your gratitude. All I want is a wife I can rely on to act like a responsible adult. I meant what I said earlier. Stay away from Fleming. If I catch you with him again you'll have more to think about than how to make the days pass faster, I can promise you!'

He was in the car and reaching for the ignition before she found her voice. It trembled with barely suppressed fury and detestation. 'If I'd realised just what kind of despotic little Hitler you really were, I'd have run a mile before letting you near either of us! I should have had my head examined for even considering looking you up!'

'But you did, and you're stuck with the situation,' he said without turning his head. 'I'll see you Friday, if not before.'

Lian stepped back away from the car as he started the engine. Her limbs felt shaky, her heart like a leaden weight inside her chest. She'd said far more than she'd intended, and with a vitriol she could hardly credit even now. And all for what? Resentment over his taking the heavy hand?

There was more to it than that, she acknowledged with a burst of honesty as the Jaguar pulled away with a harsh screeching of tyres. The whole thing had been festering ever since she had met Christine. All it had needed to erupt was an excuse. If she was right in her suspicions about the two of them, she could hardly blame him too much. Duty was one thing, personal feelings quite another. What kind of compensation could she offer him in comparison with his sister's partner?

CHAPTER SEVEN

THERE was no communication from Bryn at all until the Wednesday evening, and then just a brief telephone call to say he would be home the following afternoon.

'That was short and sweet,' commented Fiona lightly when Lian returned to the terrace after taking the call in the hall. 'A man of few words, my brother. But then, I suppose he's saving it all for when he sees you face to face.'

Lian didn't doubt it, although there had been nothing in his tone to suggest he might still be feeling the same icy anger with which he had driven away two days ago. He had sounded totally composed. Almost businesslike, in fact.

Mrs Thornley had retired indoors when the midges started biting. They didn't seem to bother Fiona, and Lian was beyond caring. It was too lovely an evening to be indoors, anyway. The sunset coming up promised to be well worth waiting for.

'Ringing from the flat, was he?' Fiona added, frowning over some figures she was working out.

Lian glanced at her sharply. 'What flat?'

'Kensington. He keeps the place as a *pied-à-terre* for when he has to stay over in town.' The other looked surprised. 'He didn't tell you?'

'No,' Lian acknowledged. She added without haste, 'I don't suppose it occurred to him.'

Her sister-in-law deposited pen and paper on the arm of her chair with a quiet deliberation. 'Things aren't going so well with you two, are they?' she said. 'You've been going around like a zombie ever since Bryn left on Monday.' She paused. 'Anything you want to talk about?'

Lian shook her head. 'Thanks, but I don't think so. It's something we have to work out for ourselves.'

There was a small silence before Fiona responded. When she did speak it was tentatively. 'I'm not trying to interfere in any way, Lian, but I've obviously known my brother a lot longer than you have. Will you believe me when I tell you he isn't as hard-headed as he sometimes appears?' Perhaps fortunately, she didn't wait for any answer. 'He'd have done better to wait a while before bringing you here. Give you both a chance to get to know one another again.'

Lian's smile held little humour. 'We never did know one another. Only in the biblical sense, and that hardly counts. If it weren't for Jonathan——' She broke off, shaking her head again. 'Not much point in saying that, is there? It's all for Jonathan. *And* he's worth it!'

Fiona studied her with a curious expression. 'You must feel *something* for Bryn.'

Lian returned her gaze unemotionally. 'I do. He's a very generous man. I spent a small fortune yesterday at Louella, and another on shoes and handbags at that new shop close by your place. I drive the kind of car most women would give their eye-teeth to own, and I don't have to worry about household bills ever. I'd say I made quite a bargain, wouldn't you?'

'I'd say you were talking through your hat,' Fiona responded bluntly. 'I'm not that lousy a judge of character. You and Bryn have a lot of catching up to do, and I don't imagine it's all that easy for either of you, but, for what it's worth, I personally think he couldn't have done any better.'

Already regretting the snide comments, Lian bit her lip. 'Thanks,' she said gruffly. 'And I'm sorry for letting go with that little lot just now. Put it down to bloody-mindedness on my part. I don't know when I'm well off.'

'Bryn must have said or done something to spark it off, so he has to bear part of the blame.' Fiona pulled a droll face. 'Men are the pits when it comes to sensitivity!'

Lian laughed, feeling better in spite of herself. 'You're surely not including your Paul in that generalisation?'

'Oh, he's no exception, believe me.' There was a suggestion of acrimony in the pronouncement. 'You'll be able to meet him at the weekend. He gets back from Spain on Friday.'

'Business trip?'

'Partly. He went to buy a new stallion for the stud. That's his business, breeding horses. And riding them too, of course. He's into show-jumping.' She got rather abruptly to her feet. 'I'm going to fix myself a gin and tonic. How about you?'

About to refuse, Lian changed her mind. Alcohol had been her downfall once, but it could also be an enlivener, and boy, did she need enlivening! To hell with Bryn for the present. 'I'll have the same,' she said.

It rained all morning on Thursday, much to Jonathan's disgust. His grandmother had refused him permission to have Samson in his room again, which disgusted him even more. His father seemed to be the only one who could countermand that decision, and he wasn't here.

In the end, he took the law into his own hands and sneaked the dog upstairs when no one was looking.

Bryn arrived home at three to find Lian locked in battle with his mother over the form of punishment appropriate to flagrant disobedience. He had been standing in the sitting-room doorway for several moments before either of them noticed him—and only then because he chose to interrupt the argument.

'I think it might be better if you both calmed down and told me what the problem is,' he said. 'I gather it's to do with Jonathan.'

Bristling with self-righteous anger, his mother gave Lian no opportunity to answer. 'He deliberately disobeyed me, and now there's a window broken. If that doesn't deserve a good spanking, I don't know what does!'

'He is *not* going to be spanked,' Lian reiterated grimly, as much for Bryn's benefit as the older woman's. 'He knows he did wrong, and he's said he's sorry. That's an end of it. You can't expect a four-year-old to be the perfect little angel all the time.'

'I expect children of any age to do as they're told,' came the sharp answer. 'Mine always did.'

'Always might be putting it a bit strongly,' observed Bryn on a dry note. 'I seem to remember being on the carpet at least once a week for some misdemeanour or other. How did the window get broken?'

'Samson crashed into it jumping for a ball,' Lian told him, holding down the belligerence his mother had aroused. 'He shouldn't have taken the dog up there in the first place, and he certainly shouldn't have been playing ball with him, but the window is already being replaced and he's been well and truly scolded and sent to bed. Isn't that enough?'

'Supposing we drop the whole subject for now,' he came back levelly. 'I'm going up to change. I'd like to think the two of you will have come to terms by the time I come down again. Having my mother and my wife at loggerheads when we're all living in the same house is no joke.'

Lian was the first to make the move after his departure. She had spoken her mind with forcefulness and scant regard for her mother-in-law's right to express *her* feelings. There was no excuse for bad manners, whatever the provocation.

'I apologise,' she said stiffly. 'I shouldn't have spoken to you the way I did.'

For a moment it seemed the other wasn't going to respond, then she nodded and turned back to the embroidery she had been working on when the row erupted. With the status quo re-established, there was no point in hanging around, Lian thought. Her company was not required.

She was almost at the door when Mrs Thornley spoke; her tone was reserved but no longer as aloof. 'I went too far myself. You were quite right to stand up to me. I think we have to start again.'

Lian's response was without hesitation. 'I'd like to.'

'Good.' A faint smile touched the stately features. 'Go and comfort your son. I'll see you both at tea.'

Mounting the stairs, Lian hoped the portents were as good as they appeared to be. It would be of considerable help if she could achieve even a minor rapport with her mother-in-law. Bryn was another matter altogether. They still had to resolve their differences wholesale.

She heard Jonathan cry out as she approached his room. It wasn't until she crashed open the door that she realised he was yelling with laughter not pain. Bryn

looked up from his seat on the bed edge with ironically
lifted brows as she paused uncertainly on the threshold.

'Looking for me?'

'I . . . no,' she said. 'I came to make sure Jonathan was
all right.'

'As the rain still coming down in stair rods outside,'
he returned, drawing another hearty chuckle from the
small, pyjama-clad figure in the bed. 'A good thing that
window got mended so fast, or you might have found
yourself flooded right out of the door and floating down
the corridor, young man. Anyway, I think you might get
dressed for tea now, and I'll go do the same.'

Lian moved aside as he came towards the door, but
he gestured for her to precede him out of the room.

'Did you think I might have taken my mother's side
and laid into him?' he asked in low but biting tones after
closing the door so that Jonathan couldn't hear. 'You
came in like a lioness after her cub!'

'If you had laid a hand on him I'd have acted like one
too,' she retorted, refusing to be put down.

His smile was grim. 'If I laid a hand on anyone round
here, it wouldn't be Jonathan. If it's of any interest at
all, I don't happen to consider spanking a child his age
a suitable chastisement either. I was thrashed too often
myself to be in favour of corporal punishment as anything but a last resort.'

'Nice to know we're in agreement on some things,'
she said, treating the implied threat with the scorn it
merited. 'I'm sorry you had to come in at that particular
moment. Your mother and I haven't been getting along
too well, though things might be about to start
improving.'

'Probably because you wouldn't let yourself be brow-
beaten by her. She admires strength of purpose, even if

she does consider it misplaced.' He was looking at her with appraisal. 'Your hair is different.'

The sudden veering of subject took her by surprise. She felt herself floundering. 'I had it styled. It's a couple of inches shorter and layered, that's all.'

'I like it.' He said it matter-of-factly, but still managed to bring a little glow to her heart. 'New dress too, isn't it? Green seems to be your colour.'

'I did as you suggested and went shopping,' she acknowledged. 'I spent a lot of money.'

'That's what it's there for.' He was obviously unperturbed by the confession. 'I imagine you're well used to the car by now?'

'Yes.' She could say that with genuine enthusiasm. 'It goes like a dream!'

His whole manner had altered, the contours of his face subtly softened. 'Come and talk to me while I change. I've had a hell of a week.'

Her heart jerked. Like this, he was so different from the man she had last seen gripping the wheel of the car as if he would have liked to do the same with her throat. Grudge-bearing was apparently outside his code of conduct. She could hardly do less than meet him halfway.

'Trouble at t'mill?' she asked lightly, moving with him along the corridor to their own room.

His laugh warmed her anew. 'You might just say that. Board meetings should be held in an arena! One of these fine days I'm going to throw in the towel and retire to my country seat like my forebears before me.'

'You'd be bored to tears inside of a few weeks,' Lian responded, not taking the statement at all seriously.

'I doubt it. Not with an estate the size of Revedon to run.' He had his back to her as he took off his jacket, his tone easy. 'I'm little more than a figurehead these days, anyway.'

Lian doubted that. A man of Bryn's ilk would never allow himself to be pushed into a back seat in any sphere. He had dropped the jacket on to the bed; she moved automatically to pick it up and shake it out prior to hanging it away in his wardrobe.

'Would there be enough work to keep two of you going?' she asked, and could have kicked herself for bringing in any reference at all to the man who had been the prime cause of the friction between them a few days ago.

If Bryn felt any resurgence of that previous reaction, he wasn't disclosing it. 'I'd be taking over the whole show,' he said levelly. 'I don't imagine Fleming would want to stay on in those circumstances, although that would remain to be seen. The law doesn't allow me to fire him without good reason.'

Lian gazed at him with suddenly widened eyes. 'You're really considering it, aren't you?'

He returned her regard, the expression in his eyes impossible to read. 'Would it put you out to have me around on a regular basis?'

'Of course not.' The reply was too swift; she made some attempt to modify the impression. 'Jonathan would be thrilled. He thinks you're the bee's knees!'

The lean features showed a fleeting though no less genuine pleasure. 'That's gratifying on such a short acquaintance. I haven't had a lot to do with children his age before.' The pause was timed, his voice acquiring a lightly mocking note. 'And do you think I'm the bee's knees too?'

Lian felt her stomach muscles begin a fluttering contraction. Her heartbeats sounded unnaturally loud in her ears. Love might be just a word so far as the two of them were concerned, but the emotions he could arouse in her were far from deficient.

'More like a hornet,' she murmured, trying to strike the right note. 'Bees can only sting once.'

His laugh held a purely masculine appreciation. 'Point taken.'

Lian made one small sound of protest as he took hold of her. 'Jonathan...'

'I took the precaution of locking the door as we came in,' he said. 'It's called planning and forethought.'

His lips nuzzled hers, teasing them apart with gentle insistence, filling her with warmth and a trembling weakness as she felt the pressure of his body so strong and hard against her softer flesh.

She kissed him back with a feverish intensity, making up for the loneliness and deprivation of the past three days and nights. It didn't matter what or why or how they were together just so long as they were together. Nothing could mar the sheer elation of being in his arms again. Nothing would be allowed to mar it—not even the memory of suspicion and uncertainty still hovering somewhere at the back of her mind. He wanted her, Lian, right now, and she wanted him too. More than she had allowed herself to realise.

With clothing removed, there was all the time in the world for rediscovery. Lying there on top of the silk bed cover, he explored her body with hands and lips and eyes. His touch fired her with a sensuality she couldn't control—didn't even try to control. She had to know him the same way, with every sense she possessed. The taste of salt on his skin was a stimulant in itself, the feel of muscle rippling beneath her fingers yet another. By the time they came together she was past all rational

thought: a vibrant, craving, wholly uninhibited partici-
pant in an act of pure glorification.

Head buried in her shoulder, breathing slowly
steadying, Bryn said softly, 'Worth every minute of
waiting, I'd say. How about you?'

The way Lian felt at the moment, she would have
preferred some less physically orientated observation, but
that was something she would just have to want. The
words 'I love you' were reserved for those who actually
did share the deeper emotion. Whether they would ever
be used between the two of them was a question without
a positive answer. Only time would tell.

'Infinitely,' she agreed. Her hands were still clutching
the broad shoulders; she could feel the grooves where
her nails had dug into his flesh during those final,
tumultuous moments. So much passion, and none of it
meaningful in any worthy sense. He could no doubt
conjure the same for any woman he took to his bed.

'Did you really have this in mind all the time?' she
asked reflectively, thinking back on what he had said.
'I mean, locking the door...'

'It was either this,' he said, 'or venting my spleen some
other way. I was in a filthy mood to start with after trying
to reconcile the warring factors round the board table
this morning. Arriving home to that hardly made my
day any brighter.' He lifted his head a little to view her
face, mouth pulling into a smile. 'Spanking you would
have afforded some satisfaction at the time, but I think
I made the right choice.'

'I thought you were against corporal punishment,' she
murmured.

'You're not four years old, and you were asking for
it.' His tone was light but there was a certain glint in the

grey eyes. 'I'll only take so much, especially when I'm out of sorts. Consider yourself warned.'

'I'd be quaking in my shoes,' she responded with saccharine sweetness, 'if I were wearing any!'

He laughed, and bent to kiss her again. 'That's what I like, a woman who knows her place!' He added with reluctance, 'I suppose we'd better show our faces downstairs for tea, or Mother's going to think we're in the throes of a major row. Let's hope Jonathan learned his lesson. I wouldn't want her to feel her authority was being taken from her in any way.'

'I'll make sure he doesn't deliberately disobey her again,' promised Lian with more hope than trust. 'I did warn you he wasn't any Little Lord Fauntleroy.'

'And thank the lord for it! I'd hate to think any son of mine was lacking in spirit.' Bryn was moving as he spoke, pressing himself to his feet to stand for a moment looking down at her without a flicker of self-consciousness over his own nudity. 'Get up,' he added gruffly, 'and stop tempting me. I'm saving myself for another day.'

Lian hoped that didn't preclude the night. Right now it was all she could think about.

They went down together. Wearing fine cord trousers and close-fitting white T-shirt, Bryn looked renewed all the way through. Lian hoped he really was seriously considering taking over the estate. Good at the job or not, Duncan Fleming didn't come across as a man to be totally trusted.

Somewhat to her surprise, Jonathan was with his grandmother. She had more than half anticipated a retreat to the staff quarters where he was likely to receive biscuits and sympathy. Mrs Thornley herself appeared to be treating the whole incident as if it had never happened. Like her son, she apparently bore no grudges.

'There was a telephone call from John Denvers,' she announced. 'I told Mrs Banks to tell him you'd call him back——' there was a ghost of a twinkle in the glance she sent Lian's way '—when you were ready.'

Bryn said something short and sharp under his breath. 'If it's what I think it is, they can stew for a while,' he stated with emphasis. 'I already made my position known.'

'So it's unlikely that you'll have to go back to town again?' his mother asked.

'Not only unlikely, but definitely out.' He took a seat at Lian's side on one of the sofas, sliding an arm companionably along the back-rest behind her head. 'In fact, I just came to a decision I've been contemplating making for some time.'

'You're taking over here?' Mrs Thornley sounded delighted. 'And not before time too! I've never cared overmuch for Duncan Fleming, as you know. He was your father's choice.' She paused there. 'How will you get rid of him?'

Bryn shrugged. 'I'll leave it entirely up to him. If he wants to stay on as my assistant, there's nothing to stop him.'

Lian was silent, hardly daring to believe that their improved relationship might have some bearing on that decision. To have Bryn here every day—and night—would be wonderful. It would give them so much more of a chance to develop some deeper, more meaningful feelings for each other.

Who was she kidding? she asked herself wryly at that point. She was in love with Bryn now. Why else would she feel so desperate at the very thought of him with another woman? From the moment of seeing his image gazing out at her from the pages of that magazine, she had been living in a dream. To have her fantasies realised the way they had been went beyond all imagining. She was his wife. No matter what Christine might or might not have meant to him, she had his name and his son, and she intended to have his love one day too.

Fiona arrived just as the tea-trolley was being brought in.

'Great timing!' she exclaimed, sinking into a chair with the look of someone more than ready for a respite. 'Thank heaven Chris is back! I've been run off my feet all week. Always happens when there's only one of us to cope.' Struck by something in the atmosphere, she looked round the circle of faces in sudden speculation. 'What gives?'

'Daddy isn't going away again,' piped up Jonathan before anyone else could answer. 'He's going to stay here and run round the state.'

'Rather more than I had in mind,' returned his parent, controlling the amusement dancing in his eyes. 'And I'm afraid it won't be quite that instant a switch. I have to tie up a lot of loose ends first.'

Jonathan came and insinuated himself ostentatiously between the two on the sofa, treating Lian to his most cherubic smile so that she wouldn't feel neglected, before turning his attention back to his father. 'Me 'n' Sam can run fast,' he declared. 'Nobody can catch us!'

'I'll bear it in mind,' promised Bryn, hanging on to his equilibrium with an obvious effort. 'I'm going to need lots of help.'

'So you finally decided to opt out of the rat race.' Fiona's tone was oddly neutral. 'That's going to surprise a lot of people.'

Christine among them? Lian wondered. If the decision really had been finalised just this afternoon, then the other couldn't know, even if they had met up in London.

Her mind skittered away from that latter possibility. From now on she considered only the positive elements in this marriage of hers. Trust would come in time.

Paul Richardson turned out to be very different from expectations. Only a couple of inches taller than Fiona herself, and wiry in build, he had an attractively open face and an easy manner which drew Lian to him immediately. His hair was the most startling thing about him. Thick and curly, it shone copper-gold under the light.

'I'm a throwback,' he claimed. 'There hasn't been hair this colour in the family for three generations. If it weren't for one obscure great-great-uncle, my mother might have had a lot of explaining to do!'

'Your mother,' said Fiona drily, 'would have tarred and feathered herself if she'd ever so much as *looked* at another man!'

'An admirable quality, fidelity,' remarked Bryn on a light note. 'Would that more people practised it.'

Tongue in cheek? Lian wondered, trying not to let the thought show on her face. Trust didn't come easily, and that was a fact.

The four of them had been swimming after a friendly game of tennis. Lian had been relieved to find the competitive element played down. It was going to be quite a while before her game recovered enough from the long lay-off to stand a chance against any concentrated attack.

Sprawled now on the poolside, with the glass roof peeled back to allow in the sun without the cool breeze, she felt relaxed in body if not wholly in mind. How could anyone not enjoy this kind of life? It was what most would consider a sinecure.

There had been no further reference to the job question since Bryn's return. No doubt he considered the subject well and truly closed. Only it wasn't. Not so far as she was concerned. He would have his day filled with the thousand and one details involved in managing the estate when he took over, but it would still leave her high and dry. Unless she could become involved herself, of course. That was an idea worth pursuing.

'I'm going in again,' said the subject of her thoughts, heaving himself to his feet. Grey eyes sought green. 'Coming?'

Nothing loath, Lian dived into the water in his wake. Her stamina was coming back by leaps and bounds; she could complete twenty lengths without difficulty now. She and Jonathan had swum every morning before breakfast while Bryn had been away. The last three, he had joined them. They were a family in every sense of the word, and it felt good.

Swimming underwater, she could see Bryn's strong brown legs as he surfaced by the far rail. On impulse, she allowed her hand to trail lightly across his thigh as she came up by his side, smiling into his eyes with mischievous intent.

'Tantalising little wretch!' he growled. 'You'll do penance for that!'

'I'm already in the water so I'll just need the bread,' she said blandly. 'If that's what you had in mind?'

His smile was slow. 'What I have in mind calls for rather more privacy than we have at the moment. A pity. I think this time you might even enjoy it.'

Lian coloured a little, remembering the one time they had been alone together here in the pool. She had learned a whole lot since then. If she could satisfy his physical needs—and there was every indication of it—she stood a chance of reaching the inner man. Loving him the way she did, she could wait.

'I think I might too,' she murmured. She waited a deliberate moment before changing the topic, aware of the frustrated gleam in the grey eyes. 'Would you say there's any chance that Fiona and Paul might eventually get married?'

'I've no idea,' Bryn admitted. 'They've been seeing each other for over eighteen months now, but they never seem to progress. Paul's too wrapped up in the horse world, I think. It doesn't leave him all that much time for romance. Fiona...' He paused, lifting his shoulders in a brief shrug. 'Who knows? She gave up confiding in me a long time ago. Why the interest, anyway?'

'Feminine curiosity,' Lian returned lightly, reluctant to admit that because she was happy she wanted everyone else to be too. She changed tack again. 'Did you tell Duncan Fleming the news yet?'

A line appeared between the dark brows. 'Yes, I did. It seemed fair to give him plenty of notice, even though it's going to be a week or two before I actually put it into effect.'

'How did he take it?'

'As one might expect.' The line had deepened a fraction. 'Feeling sorry for him?'

'I suppose,' she said reflectively, 'one has to feel a certain amount of sympathy. On the other hand, it isn't as if he'd been given the push altogether. He'll still be drawing a salary.'

'The same salary.' Bryn's tone was unwontedly brusque. 'I don't intend penalising the man.' He pushed himself away from the rail. 'Time we were getting dressed. I've a couple of phone calls to make.'

'Not business on a Sunday.' Lian kept her tone casual. 'Can't it wait till morning?'

'Time and tide wait for no man,' he responded. 'I'll see you back at the house.'

He had climbed from the pool and vanished into the changing cubicle before she reached the steps. 'You two had a row?' asked Fiona as she came out of the water.

Lian shook her head, surprised and a little perturbed. 'What makes you think we might have?'

'The look on Bryn's face just now—as if he'd swallowed bitter aloes!' The other smiled and shrugged. 'Probably got a mouthful of chlorine. I thought the pool service overdid it a bit this time. You going in too?' she asked as Lian reached for her towel and slung it around her shoulders.

'I feel a bit chilly,' Lian admitted truthfully. 'I'll be fine once I'm dried and dressed. See you both later.'

She was taking it for granted that Paul was staying to lunch, but it didn't necessarily follow. They might even have planned to go out somewhere. Not that they were going to have too much time, if so. It was already nearly half-past twelve.

Bryn was using the telephone in the hall; she could hear his voice through the opened doorway as she entered the house via the sitting-room.

'Lunch then, tomorrow. The White Hart on the Coniston road,' he said. 'I'll be there.'

That was Christine he'd been speaking to, Lian thought dully as he replaced the receiver and moved towards the stairs. Who else would he be arranging to meet in some out-of-the-way spot?

CHAPTER EIGHT

INCLUDING Jonathan, they were six to lunch. Paul was almost like one of the family, Lian thought, envying his ease of manner. Mrs Thornley approved of him too. Her whole attitude underlined the fact.

'I thought we might take a run out to Grasmere this afternoon,' said Fiona towards the end of the meal. 'You'd like to see Dove Cottage and Wordsworth's grave, wouldn't you, Lian?'

'Very much,' the latter acknowledged. 'Only there's no great rush if no one else is bothered about going.'

'Sounds a nice idea,' put in Paul amenably. 'We can call back at my place for tea. Do you like horses, Lian?'

'I've never had much to do with them,' she admitted. 'I'm afraid I don't ride at all.'

'Never too late to start. I've a nice quiet mare ideal for a beginner. You'll have to come over when you've time, and I'll put you up. Under supervision, of course.'

'I like horses,' claimed Jonathan eagerly. 'I wouldn't fall off.'

Paul laughed. 'I'll bet you wouldn't either! Pity I don't have anything small enough to take you.' To Bryn he added, 'You should think about getting him a pony. You left a section of the stables operative, didn't you?'

'That's right.' Bryn sounded agreeably disposed towards the idea. 'I plan on keeping a couple of mounts myself eventually. A pony shouldn't be much of a problem.'

Jonathan's eyes were like saucers. He could hardly believe it was true. So far he hadn't become blasé about his changed fortunes, Lian reflected, viewing his beaming little face. If she had anything at all to do with it, he never would, although the way the goodies were piling up she was going to have her work cut out. Couldn't anyone else see how damaging it could be to over-indulge a child his age?

From the expression she caught in Bryn's eyes as their glances briefly met, he knew exactly what she was thinking. What he didn't appreciate was how she felt, and why. The sudden yearning to be back in the flat she had called home for more than four years was ridiculous, but knowing it didn't stop her feeling that way. At least there her problems had only been of a financial nature, whereas here at Revedon she was in a constant state of flux.

'I think you and I should take Samson for a good long walk this afternoon, Jonathan,' said Mrs Thornley diplomatically. 'You won't want to be trailing round museums.'

The mention of Sam was all it took to oust any notion of accompanying the other party. Given the opportunity, Jonathan would willingly have shared the dog's kennel and run each night rather than be parted. Whether a pony would take precedence remained to be seen. On balance, Lian preferred the dog. Riding could be hazardous for adults, never mind small boys.

They went in Paul's Range Rover to save taking two cars. He would, he said, drive the three of them back after tea. With the two men seated in front, Lian found time and opportunity to consider the implications of what she had overheard earlier. It was going to be interesting to hear what explanation Bryn came up with

for not being home for lunch tomorrow. That was if he
bothered to give one at all. The only way to be certain
of her facts was to follow him when he went to keep this
appointment he had made, and that in itself could be
difficult. What excuse did *she* give for absenting herself
from the luncheon table?

Once past the small but lovely Rydal Water it was only
a mile or so to Grasmere. Lying in a green valley, and
almost ringed round by mountains, the lake was tranquil
in the afternoon sunlight. Dove Cottage looked exactly
the way Lian had pictured it with its white walls and
diamond-paned windows. The poet's old clock still ticked
away the minutes.

After visiting the museum next door, they found the
site of the Wishing Gate on the old road running along
the east shore.

Drinking in the beautiful views, Lian was vitally aware
of Bryn standing at her back—so close she could feel
the warmth radiating from his body. The feel of his hands
coming to rest on her shoulders made her quiver. There
would never, she was sure, come a time when his touch
failed to stir her.

'"We drank tea the night before I left Grasmere, on
the island in that lovely lake",' he quoted softly. 'I
wonder if Coleridge would find it much altered now from
the way it was then?'

'Apart from the trippers, you mean?' asked Fiona with
a seemingly deliberate wrecking of mood. 'It was a
mistake to come on a Sunday. I don't imagine we'll even
get near the churchyard, much less the grave!'

'I can always come back another time,' said Lian. 'It
would be nice to see the village when it's less busy.'

'In which case, we'll make tracks for Long Acres,'
said Paul. 'I'm more than ready for a drink.'

Bryn moved up on his sister as the four of them made their way back to where they had left the car. Lian couldn't hear what he said, but it brought a spark to Fiona's eyes and a short reply. Paul seemed oblivious of any atmosphere; Lian had the impression that his mind was on his horses. If Fiona's present mood had anything at all to do with that preoccupation, it seemed that her feelings for the man might go somewhat deeper than she had cared to admit.

Long Acres lay towards Hawkshead. Seeing the signs for Coniston, Lian kept an eye open for the pub Bryn had mentioned on the phone, to be rewarded with a sighting just before they turned off down another, narrower road. At least she would know which way to come should she decide to follow her inclination. She had to think long and hard before she made that decision.

Paul's home was a lovely old barn of a place. It had a sizeable stable block set around a paved courtyard, and several acres of pasture. Apart from his breeding stock, he kept a string of four jumpers, with which he spent more than half the year travelling to the various shows. Neither he nor his horses were quite good enough to make the very top grade, he told Lian, but he enjoyed the life. The stud was run by his assistant while he was away.

Bryn was obviously drawn to the big black stallion called Star who lived the life of Reilly in between serving the mares sent from all over the country for his attention. The two of them were alike in many ways, reflected Lian, watching Bryn rub the velvety nose after quietening the spirited creature with a few soft words: both of them big and dark and unpredictable, with an element of danger always present. She would almost rather tackle the horse than the man in certain circumstances.

'If it's a stallion you're fancying for yourself, I know of a five-year-old grey that would be exactly right for you,' said Paul from the stable door. 'His present owner is finding him a bit too much of a handful, but I don't think you'd have any trouble. How about I arrange for you to see him?'

'Worth a look,' agreed the other. 'You might keep an eye open for a suitable pony for Jonathan. I'll want a good steady mare too.'

'If you're thinking of me, I'm not all that sure I'm bothered about learning to ride,' disclaimed Lian, and then hastily, 'Of course, Fiona might want——'

'I don't have time,' stated the latter flatly. 'Not on any regular basis, anyway. If we've finished the tour, I wouldn't mind getting on home. I've one or two things I must see to before tomorrow.'

'Of course.' Paul's face was suddenly shuttered. 'I left the car keys in the house. I'll go get them.'

Bryn came out from the stable as the younger man departed. Closing the lower half of the door again, he said equably, 'If you resent his way of life so much, why bother seeing him? He isn't going to give it up for you.'

'Did I ever suggest I might want him to?' came the tart response. 'The trouble with you, Bryn, is you read too much into too little.'

'Is that a fact?' He sounded mockingly amused. 'I'd have said the writing was on the wall. The sacrifice is going to have to come from you, if anyone at all. One of the crosses you women have to bear.'

'For which we gain what?' she retorted.

'The love of a good man, in your case. You'd have a hard job finding one better.' Just for the moment his eyes met Lian's, an indecipherable expression in their grey depths, then he was looking at his sister again. 'There are always compensations.'

Such as the ones *he* found with her, thought Lian hollowly. Lucky for him she hadn't turned out to be a reluctant pupil. If they had nothing else, they had a great sex life!

It was a long and quiet evening. Bryn spent over an hour of it up in the study. Doing what, Lian had no idea and didn't care to ask. From what he had said on Friday, he would still have to spend some time away tidying up his affairs before turning in his badge. Not that it was going to be a total severance, in any case, as he would still retain an interest in all the companies. They would simply become a source of income without the physical involvement.

He emerged around ten to find her sitting out alone on the terrace with the lights switched off so as not to attract the insect nightlife.

'Your mother went up about twenty minutes ago,' she said in answer to his query. 'I haven't seen Fiona since shortly after you went upstairs.'

'Thoughtless of them both to leave you on your own,' he commented.

'I don't see why,' she countered. 'I'm supposed to be family, not a guest.'

'You *are* family. Make no mistake about that.' He had taken the seat his mother had recently vacated, his white silk shirt a beacon in the darkness. 'I wonder why it is,' he remarked idly, 'that the nights always seem to start drawing in faster than the days drew out?'

'Probably because you're looking forward to the longer days but dreading the dark evenings,' Lian answered without thinking, and felt his glance.

'Is that what you did?'

'I haven't enjoyed winters very much for several years,' she admitted. 'I'm sure it's going to be very different here.'

'I can promise you that,' said Bryn. 'The house is closed to the public from the middle of October, which means it's open to friends. We'll have to organise some dinner parties for you to meet people.'

It wasn't what she had meant, but she let it pass. Sitting here like this in the dark, she could almost feel content with her lot. All she needed was the assurance that it wasn't Christine whom Bryn was meeting tomorrow. Not such a lot to ask.

'Are you planning on going in to the office in the morning?' she asked on what she hoped was a casual note. 'Or are you leaving it all for the day you actually take over?'

'As a matter of fact,' he said, equally casually, 'I'll be out from around eleven. A luncheon appointment. I should be back by three, so there'll still be time to run over to Lindale to see the pony Paul telephoned about earlier. It's a six-year-old, and well used to children, so it should be ideal for Jonathan. He'll come too, of course.'

Lian was only half listening. Four hours was surely a long time to spend over a meal? Unless lunch was only the prelude to other diversions, of course. The pub had looked big enough to have rooms to let. Perhaps...

She stopped the thought right there with wry purpose. She was building this whole case on the flimsiest of evidence and not one shred of real proof. Hardly the way to cement their relationship into a firm foundation. She had to give him the benefit of the doubt until proved otherwise.

'I'm going to have a nightcap,' he said now. 'How about you?'

Lian shook her head. 'I'm fine, thanks.'

'I know.' His voice was suddenly softer, and infinitely disturbing. 'In fact, I think I might pass up the drink and go straight to bed.'

Her heartbeats were thudding in her ears, but suspicion still played too great a part for any kind of dissemblance. 'Can't you think of anything else but sex?' she asked shortly.

It was too dark to see his features clearly, though there was no doubting the change in his tone. 'Not at the moment, no. Are you going to oblige me, or do I have to assert my rights?'

She came upright in the chair with a jerk. 'What *rights*?'

He hadn't moved a muscle himself. 'As your husband, I'm entitled to expect a certain compliance, if nothing else.'

The intimation that she had provided no more than the former hurt as nothing had hurt before. She had given him her all. What more could he ask?

'You're still living in the dark ages,' she retorted with bitter sarcasm. 'Wives aren't chattels to be used at will any more! I married you because of Jonathan, not to become a glorified concubine!'

'A concubine would know which side her bread was buttered,' came the taut response. 'Jonathan isn't the only one to gain from the arrangement.'

'Oh, I see.' Lian was too incensed to care what she said. 'You think a car and a new wardrobe adequate payment for services rendered. If that's the case, you can have the lot back. I don't want anything you can offer me, Bryn—grudgingly or otherwise. I'm my own person, and I'll stay that way!'

The pause stretched for what seemed an age. She could almost taste the tension in the air. With her temper cooling, she found herself horrified at how far this whole thing had gone. In the space of a few moments they had destroyed everything they had managed to achieve over the past few weeks.

'Bryn——' she began hesitantly, but he cut her off with a curt gesture.

'I think we both said more than enough. I'm going to get that drink.'

Lian sat motionless and aching as he went back into the house. Hard and hurtful words between husband and wife could normally be cancelled out, or at least glossed over, with an apology and a loving kiss, but where the love itself wasn't shared the making up was no simple task. And all because of one phone call.

There was a little bit more to it than just that though, she told herself defensively. It could have been pure coincidence that Christine was away from the shop at the same time that Bryn had been in London, but, taken in total with everything else, it seemed more and more unlikely. Why should he discard the lovely blonde if she was willing to accept the situation as it stood? And why should he not enjoy what time he could of their own enforced union at the same time. To a man, the act itself required no emotional commitment.

He didn't come outside again, and there was no sign of him when she finally stirred herself to go indoors. In all probability he had taken his drink up to the study where he could think things over and decide on a course of action. That action of some kind would be taken, she had no doubt at all. Bryn wasn't the kind to simply ignore what had passed between them. His male pride alone would need appeasement.

She was in bed before he put in an appearance. Feigning sleep, she lay listening to his movements as he undressed. A further appeal for amnesty between them might be propitious if she could only bring herself to make the effort.

The words remained unsaid for the reason that she couldn't come up with any that sounded right. His emergence from the bathroom, and subsequent approach to the bed found her no nearer a solution to the problem.

She held her breath when he slid between the sheets, releasing it on a gasp as he pulled her roughly over on to her back. With his bedside lamp still lit she could see the cold anger in his eyes, the tautness of his jawline.

The fine silk of her nightdress ripped like paper to the savage pull of his hand. Steel-like fingers roved her body without finesse as he kissed her long and hard and stiflingly on the lips. Lian felt her senses swimming, her limbs losing all use. She was unable to utter a word when he suddenly rolled away from her.

Lying rigidly still on his back with breath coming hard and heavy, he said harshly, '*That's* what it's like to be used.'

Her voice came low and ragged. 'You can't treat me that way, Bryn. Not if you want me to stay. And if I go, Jonathan goes with me.'

'Don't count on it,' he said. 'He's my son, and he isn't leaving. What you do is your own affair. I'll see you don't lose out financially.'

Blind rage brought her surging upright to swing a clenched fist at his uncaring face. The fierce satisfaction as she connected with the hard male cheekbone overrode the pain in her knuckles. One blow was all she managed before his hand shot out and gripped her wrist.

'I never hit a woman in anger in my life,' he gritted, 'but there's a first time for everything!'

'Go ahead, why don't you?' she invited recklessly. 'One more experience to chalk up!'

Kneeling over him, her hair tumbled about her face and eyes blazing defiance, she was oblivious to her own semi-nudity until she saw his gaze drop to her bared breasts and subtly alter expression. Anger was replaced by repulsion at the very thought of being subjected to that same debasement again. She pushed herself swiftly away, clutching the remains of her nightdress about her.

'Don't even consider it—unless you want the whole household to know what's happening!'

'Including Jonathan?' His voice held hard derision. 'Don't fret, I've no intention of repeating myself. Not tonight, at any rate. I'd suggest you lie down and get to sleep if you don't want to experience the alternative. I'm just about at the limit with you, Lian!'

'That makes two of us,' she responded, but she was already sliding back down between the sheets. The torn nightdress would have to stay until morning because there was no way she was discarding the remains with Bryn watching.

He turned out the lamp before settling down on his side with his back to her. Bare moments later, or so it seemed, his deeper, even breathing told her he was asleep. And that was as much as all this meant to him, she thought hollowly. She was the only one who hurt.

The other pillow was empty when she opened her eyes again. Memory brought a rush of depression and misery. No horrible dream, but reality in all its stark detail. There could be no way back to where they were at this time yesterday. They'd both seen to that.

It was still only a little after six o'clock, she realised. Wherever Bryn had gone, it could only be because he didn't want to be here when she awoke. He might even be making an early call to Christine. A bruised ego needed reassurance.

Her own bruising went far deeper than that—both physically and emotionally. Love and hate were closely related; she was just beginning to appreciate that fact. Bryn could be cruel in anger. Ruthless too. What she couldn't afford was for him to guess just how much he had hurt her last night. That would be playing right into his hands.

Showered, and dressed in peach linen, she went along to Jonathan's room at seven with the intention of telling him they were giving swimming a miss for today. Finding his bed empty was a blow for which she wasn't prepared. There was only one other person he could be with at this hour, and that was Bryn. Stealing a march on her in retaliation for what she had put him through last night, no doubt.

One thing she refused to do was make Jonathan a bone for the two of them to scrap over, she thought determinedly. She might have threatened to do so last night, but that had been in the heat of the moment, not calculated the way this was. Having married Bryn for Jonathan's sake in the first place, she had to stick with it regardless. No running away the moment the going got tough.

One thing she could do, she decided on the way downstairs, was ascertain just how much truth there really was in her suspicions over Christine. If that meant following him this lunchtime, then that was what she

would do. She could always pretend she was going into
Kendal to do some shopping and would be having lunch
out. There was no reason at all why that should be
thought peculiar.

Seated close by the side window in the sitting-room,
flipping idly and unseeingly through a magazine, she saw
Bryn and Jonathan returning from the pool. Bryn was
carrying the small, chuckling figure on his shoulders with
his hands clasped lightly over the boy's knees to keep
him from falling backwards. They were so much alike
that it brought a lump to Lian's throat. What she had
to avoid, she thought painfully, was allowing Jonathan
to acquire his father's less worthy characteristics as he
grew up.

Mrs Thornley was down by eight o'clock as always.
Breakfast was at half-past eight. The two of them were
already seated when Bryn and Jonathan arrived. Forcing
herself to return the former's gaze, Lian couldn't restrain
a slight gasp as she took in the purple bruise below his
right eye.

'What on earth have you done?' asked his mother in
startled tones.

'Walked into a door,' he returned levelly. 'It happens
to the best of us.' The eyes still holding Lian's were
devoid of expression. 'Enjoy your lie-in? It seemed a
shame to waken you from a sound sleep just for a swim.'

'Thoughtful of you,' she said without inflexion.

Mrs Thornley gave them both a sharp look, but refrained from any comment. She would have had to be
both blind and totally insensitive to be unaware of the
atmosphere, Lian conceded. Of them all, only Jonathan
was his normal happy little self.

'I can swim right across the pool now,' he announced
proudly. 'I'm going to be in the 'lympics when I'm big

enough.' His voice took on an even greater enthusiasm. 'Daddy says we can go and see a pony this afternoon!'

'Really?' Try as she might, Lian could conjure no brighter response. 'Providing he's back in time, of course.'

'I'll be back.' It was said with quiet certainty. 'A promise is a promise.'

It was Mrs Thornley who got round the momentary silence with a tactful change of subject. What she was thinking, Lian couldn't begin to guess and told herself she didn't care. Bryn had no right to tell Jonathan about the pony without her say-so. Four and a half wasn't nearly old enough to begin riding lessons. He could so easily fall and break his neck.

Bryn retired to the study almost immediately after the meal, murmuring something about having some papers to sort. Lian gave him no more than twenty minutes before bracing herself for a renewal of hostilities. No more kowtowing: from now on she would go all out for self-assertion. Let him find out the hard way that she wasn't about to be relegated to any back seat in this family.

He was seated at the desk with an open file in front of him when she entered the room. For a moment his expression remained abstracted, as if his mind was still on whatever it was he was studying so assiduously, then the lean features reset into cold, hard lines.

'Did it occur to you to knock?' he enquired stonily.

'No,' Lian admitted. 'I leave that kind of thing to the staff.' She paused, fighting to retain a certain detachment from the emotions seething inside her. 'I don't want Jonathan to ride just yet. He isn't old enough. Perhaps in a year or two he——'

'Why wait till now?' The question was clipped. 'You had every chance to object yesterday when the subject came up.'

'With Jonathan right there and all starry-eyed? What kind of a spoil-sport would I have been made to look?'

'The same kind you'll look now, if you try to stop him having a pony of his own.'

'Ah, but I'm not going to be the one putting paid to the idea,' she returned. 'You started it, you can end it. He'll be disappointed, naturally, but he'll get over it. Children have short memories.'

Bryn hadn't risen from his seat, nor made any move at all other than the initial lifting of his head. He sat there now just gazing at her for a lengthy moment with contempt in his eyes.

'You really think I'm going to go back on my word just to placate your jealousy?' he said. 'The very reason you brought him to me was because I could give him things you couldn't—remember?'

Lian went cold and then hot. 'This isn't jealousy,' she said between her teeth. 'I happen to be concerned for his safety—something *you* don't appear to have considered. He's never been on anything bigger than a donkey, and even that only twice.'

'What did you imagine I was planning to do?' asked Bryn with irony. 'Put him up there and say get to it? He'll have someone with him the whole time.'

'No, he won't, because it isn't going to happen!' She was past restraint, intent only on getting her way. 'No pony, and that's final!'

He moved then, swinging the swivel-chair to get slowly and purposefully to his feet. Lian stood her ground as he came round the desk towards her, though there was no denying the sudden trembling weakness in her limbs.

If he laid so much as a finger on her he would be sorry. She would make it her business to let his mother know exactly what kind of man her son really was!

'You,' he said grimly, reaching her, 'are just about at the end of your rope!'

Two hands like vices fastened on her upper arms, dragging her up on her toes to meet his mouth. The kiss was merciless, punishing—yet it still elicited a spark deep within her. She had to fight not to respond to him. It took everything she had to meet his eyes without flinching when he finally released her.

His expression underwent a sudden change as he looked at her, the anger giving way to something less easily defined.

'This is ridiculous!' he said gruffly. 'Lian——'

'I don't think there's anything much left to say,' she got out. 'Are you going to tell Jonathan?'

His jaw tautened again. 'No, I'm not. And neither are you. I'll be taking him to see the pony at three o'clock. Whether you come too is entirely your choice. Now, if you don't mind, I've got work to do.'

He was back behind the desk and sliding into his seat before she could bring herself to make any move. Short of removing Jonathan from the estate altogether—and with nowhere to go, that was hardly feasible—Lian was left with little alternative but to accept the situation as it stood. She was losing control of her son to this man she had imagined she loved, and there was not a thing she could do about it.

CHAPTER NINE

WALKING out of the study without giving way to the anger and resentment she felt was one of the hardest things Lian had ever done. Words were obviously not going to move Bryn.

So she would find a weapon to use against him. If he was indeed meeting Christine this lunchtime, it would at least be something to hold over him. His mother's and sister's regard was important to him; they were probably the only two people he cared about with any real depth. Add Jonathan to that, came the rider. She might not agree with his manner of showing it, but there was no disputing his feelings for his son—or Jonathan's for him either, if it came to that.

He was right about the jealousy, of course. She'd never had to share before. She would have got over it in time, but things were different now. She didn't want to share anything ever again with him!

Mrs Thornley received the news of her intended trip into town without comment. Jonathan, she said, would be just fine. They might even go out themselves for a run in the Daimler—with Banks to drive, of course.

Clad in a lightweight suit in a fine tan and cream stripe, Lian was out of the house and away within fifteen minutes. Kendal first, in order to pass on an hour or so before making her way out to the White Hart. There had been a garden centre fronted by a car park right across the road, she remembered. She could sit in there and keep watch on the hotel forecourt.

With no conscious intention to pay a call on Fiona, she nevertheless found her feet taking her in the direction of the shop. The sight of Christine in the window gave rise to sudden doubt, swiftly thrust aside. There was still plenty of time for the woman to keep the appointment.

Fiona's greeting was a little constrained. She quite often left the house before breakfast time, so Lian had thought nothing of it when she was absent from the table this morning, but she looked as if *she* hadn't had much sleep last night either.

'We've a load of new stock coming in this afternoon,' she said, 'so things are a bit hectic. Help yourself to coffee. It's freshly made.'

Lian did so, steeling herself to meet Christine's eyes as the other stepped from the window. 'Hello again,' she said levelly.

'Hello.' As before, the smoothly perfect features showed no friendliness. Lian wondered how Fiona could work in partnership with such an ice maiden—although it was possible that the ice was only extended in her own direction, she supposed.

'That's the display sorted out,' Christine said now, moving to pour herself a cup of the coffee. 'Shall you be able to cope with the rest?'

'Of course.' Fiona sounded as if she were thinking of something else entirely. She pulled herself up to add, 'Are you planning on coming back in, or going straight home?'

'I'm not sure. Depends when the lot we're interested in comes up. If it's after three-thirty, then it won't be worth my coming back in.'

Lian said lightly, 'Going to another auction?'

The answer came without an accompanying glance, and with no underlying inflexion. 'That's right. Whether

I'll get the piece I'm after this afternoon is something else. I'll be up against a lot of competition.'

Nothing there to arouse suspicion, Lian conceded, but she was sure all the same. This auction at which a certain item might or might not be secured was just a mite too convenient. 'Sorry,' would be tomorrow's excuse, 'I got pipped at the post!'

'I suppose I'd better get going myself,' Lian said, replacing her empty cup in its saucer. 'Thanks for the coffee.'

'Nice of you to drop in.' The smile Fiona summoned was lacking its normal warmth and vivacity. 'Have fun!'

Her sister-in-law's mood was definitely connected with Paul, Lian decided, hurrying back to where she had left the car. That made two of them with emotional problems, if stemming from rather different causes. Men were the source of most female ills when it all boiled down.

She made it back to the street where the shop was situated just in time to see Christine getting into the white Rover parked outside. Following at a safe distance with two other cars between them, she saw the Rover head out on the road for Windermere, and knew a sense of vindication mingled with dolour at having her theory proved. That was no auction for which the other was heading, but an assignation with the man she had wanted for herself.

There was no sign of the Rover after Clappersgate, only that hardly mattered because Lian knew where it was going. She supposed it was pretty pointless, in actual fact, to continue following, but she kept on doing it anyway. She might even consider walking in on the pair of them just to show them she wasn't quite the kind of fool they took her for. It would almost be worth it to see the look on Bryn's face when he realised they were rumbled.

Who was she trying to kid? she asked herself ruefully at that point. Nothing could be worth the kind of heartache she was experiencing right now. All very well to tell herself she hated Bryn, but it wasn't that simple. He was her husband, and Jonathan's father, and while the one could be altered, the other couldn't, so she had better face up to the long-term prospect.

She was about half a mile from her destination when the engine cut out. Fortunately, there was very little traffic on the road at the time and she managed to trickle the car into the edge before momentum ran out altogether. The petrol gauge told its own story. She had meant to fill up on the way into town earlier, but with her mind on other matters she had totally forgotten about it.

So now what did she do? Lian asked herself wryly. It could be twenty miles to the next petrol station for all she knew. The nearest place with a public telephone seemed likely to be the White Hart itself. Hardly suitable unless she wanted to run the risk of being seen by Bryn or Christine.

Flagging down a passing motorist seemed the only alternative solution, if not exactly a recommended exercise for a woman on her own. Once she reached a garage, she could organise a rescue service of some kind.

Sliding from behind the wheel, Lian moved to the front of the car where she could see oncoming traffic in both directions and still be reasonably safe from any mad Harry who cut the corner too fine. The driver of the Citroën approaching from the Hawkshead side was swift to respond to her signal. It wasn't until the vehicle pulled over to a stop a few feet away that she recognised the man at the wheel.

'Surprise, surprise!' said Duncan Fleming, getting out of the car. 'Didn't expect to see *you* out here. Having engine trouble?'

'I ran out of petrol,' Lian confessed sheepishly. 'I don't suppose you carry a spare can around, by any chance?'

'Not a full one. Too much of a fire hazard.' To do him credit, he was displaying none of the masculine indulgence so often devoted to such occasions when a woman was involved. 'There's a garage a couple of miles back. Lock the car up and I'll run you in.'

It would be just as easy if he went and fetched the petrol himself while she waited here, Lian thought, but it seemed churlish to say so. It shouldn't take long, anyway.

Seated beside him, she was conscious of a certain grimness in the set of the rugged features. He revved the engine with what she thought was quite unnecessary force in turning the car about. If she was making him late for some appointment or other, she was sorry, but it was just one of those things. He would be on his way again inside fifteen minutes.

The White Hart loomed into view round the next bend. Lian had time for no more than a brief scan of the cars parked out front, but the black XJ40 stood out like a beacon. Of the white Rover there was no sign, though the parking area ran round to the rear of the building, so that didn't mean it wasn't there.

'Joining him for lunch, are you?' asked Duncan, bringing her head round again with a jerk.

'Sorry?'

'That was Bryn's car at the pub, wasn't it?' There was an odd inflexion to his voice.

'It was like it. I couldn't see the registration.' She added hastily. 'I'm just out for the drive. I'm not sure where Bryn was going.'

'No, well, you wouldn't be, would you?' He paused, slanting a glance her way. 'I don't suppose he tells you much at all.'

He was right about that, Lian thought, but she wasn't about to admit it. 'It depends on what it's about,' she said lightly. 'I don't have any hand in his business interests.'

'Pure decoration, eh?' This time the glance held an open insolence. 'Can't say I blame him for taking you on. I'll bet you're a real little raver under the surface. The quiet ones usually are!'

They were coming up to the garage now. Otherwise, Lian would have insisted he stopped the car and let her out regardless. 'I'll make my own arrangements from here,' she said tautly as he brought the Citroën to a halt on the forecourt. 'And if you know what's good for you, you'll keep your opinions to yourself from now on!'

His shrug suggested total indifference. 'No skin off my nose. See you around.'

Trembling with suppressed anger, she turned towards the garage offices as he drove off the way they had come. She couldn't even gain satisfaction by telling Bryn what had been said because it would mean admitting to being out here in the first place. Duncan Fleming was an obnoxious man, without one redeeming feature. One could only hope Bryn's theory would be proved correct in that he would refuse to stay on as assistant controller.

She was back at the house by half-past two. Jonathan came running out as soon as he heard the car turn into the courtyard.

'Daddy didn't come back yet,' he said anxiously. 'Will they sell my pony to someone else if I don't go to see it?'

'No, of course not,' Lian assured him, relinquishing any lingering notion she might have had of defying Bryn's directive in the face of such eager enthusiasm. She would just have to steel herself to the idea. Perhaps if she learned to ride herself, it might help.

The sound of another engine brought an added shine to the small face. Young as he was, he could recognise the XJ40's distinctive note. Bryn turned the car in through the wide gateway and came to a halt some few yards away from where the two of them stood waiting, sitting for a brief moment just looking at them through the side window before switching off the ignition and getting out.

'Sam's in his kennel,' Jonathan announced. 'I told him about the pony and he doesn't mind.'

His father's smile lacked spontaneity. 'That's good. Give me a few minutes to change, and we'll get off.' His glance shifted to the solitary garment bag in Lian's hand. 'Not a lot to show for a morning's shopping.'

'There's not an awful lot of scope in Kendal,' she responded. 'I just about exhausted Louella's stock last time.'

'You'll have to take a trip down to Manchester,' he said. 'Are you coming with us?'

'Of course.'

His lips twisted. 'Not to be trusted with him alone, am I?'

'It's not like that at all,' Lian protested, and knew it was exactly like that, and it had to stop. Whatever his faults, Bryn was a responsible adult. He would allow no harm to come to his son. 'I'd like to see the pony too,' she tagged on lamely.

Bryn made no further comment. He seemed in an odd mood altogether, Lian thought, accompanying him indoors with Jonathan skipping on ahead. Guilt, perhaps? Strange, though, that he'd curtailed the rendezvous. It was still only twenty minutes to three.

'Hope you had a good lunch,' he said as they mounted the stairs. 'We'll be missing tea.' He added casually, 'Where did you eat?'

'The Woolpack,' she hazarded, naming the only hotel in Kendal that she could remember the name of. The lies were piling up on both sides; why should *she* feel any special guilt? 'I called in on Fiona,' she added with deliberation. 'Christine had another auction to attend this afternoon. She certainly gets out and about, doesn't she?'

'Someone has to do the buying.' His tone was devoid of expression.

They reached the bedroom in silence. Going to her walk-in wardrobe, Lian sorted out a pair of trousers in beige cotton, along with a matching shirt. Bryn came to stand in the doorway, trapping her inside the suddenly claustrophobic little room. His face was grim.

'I saw you with him,' he stated. 'I was on my way out to the car for some papers I'd forgotten to take in with me when you drove past the White Hart at Hawkshead earlier.'

Lian gazed back in stunned comprehension. So that was it! He actually thought *she* was playing away!

'I ran out of petrol,' she said. 'Duncan just happened to be passing, and took me to the nearest garage, that's all.'

'Convenient.' There was no give at all in the lean, hard features. 'Was this before or after your lunch at the Woolpack?'

Her colour came and went. 'Neither,' she confessed. 'I didn't eat lunch.'

'In other words, you lied just now. And I'm supposed to believe this fabrication about running out of petrol?' His tone was clipped, the grey eyes like flint. 'I told you to stay away from Fleming!'

Righteous anger came to her rescue. Her own eyes blazed like emeralds as she squared up to him. 'The same way *you* stayed away from Christine?'

Dark brows drew together. For a moment he seemed almost at a loss for words. When he did speak it was on a quite different note. 'Where does Christine come into the picture?'

'When did she go out of it?' Lian retorted. 'The two of you were involved before I came on the scene; I don't flatter myself that I'm an adequate substitute. She was with you in London, wasn't she? And again this lunchtime. I heard you arranging it on the phone yesterday, so don't bother trying to deny it!'

Bryn was looking at her as if he'd never seen her properly before. 'You heard me arranging to meet someone, yes. What made you so sure it was Christine?'

'I already told you, I know all about the two of you. Or are you going to try making out I'm wrong about that too?'

He shook his head. 'I don't have any reason to deny it. Neither do I have any intention of discussing it. What concerns me right now is what *you've* been up to. And don't give me any more of that ''just happened to be passing'' guff either. The arm of coincidence only stretches so far!'

'It happens to be the truth,' she said. 'If you want the full story, I followed Christine from town when she set off to meet you—just to make sure I was right. I forgot to fill up first, so I didn't quite reach the White Hart.' She was doing her best to keep her voice on an even pitch. 'I've no idea what Duncan Fleming was doing out there, but he did just happen along at the right moment. He took me to a garage in Hawkshead.'

Bryn was leaning a shoulder against the door-jamb, a sardonic slant to his upper lip. 'You're saying you had Christine's car in your sights the whole time?'

That gave Lian pause for a moment, but only for a moment. 'Long enough to be quite certain where she was going,' she declared. 'I suppose you'd like me to believe the auction was being held out that direction!'

'The auction,' he said, 'was at Little Langdale. Fiona mentioned it yesterday. You turned left at Clappersgate. Christine would have carried straight on.'

This time the pause was longer. Lian made a valiant attempt to marshal her reserves. 'As you said—convenient. You must take me for a fool, Bryn!'

'I'm not sure *what* to take you for,' he returned coldly. 'Trust cuts both ways. We'll leave the whole subject for the time being. Jonathan will be up here looking for us if we don't get a move on.'

You started it, she wanted to say, but he was already moving away. She swallowed thickly, thinking back over what he had said. She hadn't seen the white Rover again after Clappersgate, it was true. Only that didn't prove anything. If he wouldn't believe her, why should she believe him?

He was in the bathroom when she emerged from the wardrobe. His jacket and trousers had been dropped on the bed. Lian hung both items away, then changed into the trousers and shirt and ran a quick brush over her hair. Her face in the mirror looked pinched and pale, her eyes dark. She felt totally at odds with herself.

The opening of the bathroom door sent a surge of sheer desperation through her. This couldn't go on, it just couldn't! She could see Bryn reflected in the mirror, dressed now in jeans and T-shirt. His face was set in lines that discouraged communication. Nevertheless, she had to try.

'Bryn,' she began huskily, 'I——'

'Leave it,' he said with authority. 'I've a promise to keep.'

They went downstairs together, with light years between them. Jonathan was dancing with impatience. It would soon be bedtime, he complained. Bryn laughed, and scooped him up on to his shoulders to carry him out to the car, leaving Lian to follow on behind like some unwelcome third party. She was almost tempted to cry off from the trip, except that it would be difficult to explain her change of mind to Jonathan.

Bryn opened the front passenger door for her with his customary unstudied courtesy, then went round to slide behind the wheel without a further glance in her direction. Lian recalled the very first time the three of them had driven away from Revedon together. She hadn't known then what his intentions had been, but deep down she had hoped; she could admit that now. Only nothing was turning out the way she had hoped, and probably never would. Easier all round if she reconciled herself to that fact.

The farm where they were to view the pony was near Lindale. Even Lian was forced to admit that the stocky little Shetland appeared docile enough. Jonathan insisted on getting into the saddle the proper way via the stirrup, although Bryn gave him a boost from the rear. Led around the stable yard a couple of times, he soon got the feel of it.

'A natural,' said the farmer, already certain of the sale. 'Should last him a year or so depending on how he grows, then he'll need a good Exmoor or Welsh. Rory here has seen three of mine through. I dare say he'll last out another three!'

Not much hope of that, thought Lian despondently. The way things were, another child was out of the question.

Was it? asked a small voice at the back of her mind, and her throat closed up. It was true that neither she nor Bryn had taken any precautions against that happening; she simply hadn't considered the possibility.

So would it be such a bad thing if she did turn out to be pregnant? It might even draw them closer together. At best, Christine could never be more than a 'bit on the side' as the saying went. It was up to her, Lian, to make sure that Bryn had no need of anyone else.

With arrangements made to have the pony brought over to Revedon the following morning, they went back to the car trailing a reluctant Jonathan, who feared the animal might vanish into thin air overnight. Bryn was able to pacify him by suggesting they went and looked at the stable where the pony would be kept when he wasn't out to pasture. The tack bought along with the Shetland would do for the time being, he added, but they would be having a new saddle made to order.

'You're far too generous,' Lian murmured, and received a level glance.

'I've a lot of lost time to make up for.'

It being a Monday, the café utilising the major part of the old stable block was closed. Bryn drove around to the rear of the block where four loose-boxes had been preserved from the dozen or more originals, along with a small section of the cobbled courtyard cut off from the rest by a newly erected stone wall.

A young man introduced as Joe Baxter's brother, Ray, was already installed as stable-hand. He was delighted to hear that his first charge would be arriving forthwith.

'I'll be taking a look at a five-year-old stallion in the morning,' Bryn told him. 'He's supposed to be a bit of a handful.'

'Never met a stallion worth anything that wasn't,' came the cheerful reply. 'I'll be ready for him, Mr Thornley.'

'Why buy a stallion in the first place if they're so unruly?' asked Lian on the way over to the house, trying to show some interest in the equestrian avocation. 'A gelding would surely be a safer choice?'

Bryn's mouth took on a sardonic slant. 'Call it an inherent aversion to the basic idea. Anyway, I doubt if my safety is of any great concern.'

Lian swallowed on the hard little lump in her throat. 'Of course it's of concern! I shouldn't want anything to happen to you.'

'You'd be very well taken care of if it did,' he returned. 'Jonathan is my heir, but he'd need you to see him through to the time when he'd take over Revedon himself.'

'Don't talk like that,' she said thickly. 'There's nothing going to happen!'

Broad shoulders lifted briefly. 'There's no certainty in anything. If today proved nothing else, it proved that much.'

'How can *I* be your hair, Daddy?' piped up Jonathan
on a puzzled note. 'You've got lots and lots on your
head!'

The laughter glossed over an awkward moment. She
was certain of one thing, Lian thought hollowly, listening
to Bryn explaining the difference: regardless of everything and anything, she loved this man. If he never felt
the same way about her, she would have to learn to live
with it, that was all.

Mrs Thornley wanted to hear all about the pony. Bryn
left the three of them to it, and went off to the study.
At five o'clock, Jonathan had his usual light supper,
then had another hour in which to play until his bath-
time at six-thirty. By seven-fifteen he was tucked up in
bed, tired, but ecstatically happy in anticipation of the
morning. The face he turned up to Bryn when the latter
came in to say goodnight was worshipful.

'You're too big to ride Rory,' he declared judiciously,
'but you'll soon have a pony of your own, Daddy. Can
Mummy have one too?'

'If she wants one,' Bryn replied. 'You'll have to talk
her into it.'

Outside in the corridor, he said, 'It's up to you, of
course, but you might enjoy it if you gave it a chance.'

Lian didn't look at him. 'As an alternative to a job,
you mean?'

'As a hobby.' The pause held weight. 'If you're still
intent on a job, one of the guides will be leaving us in
a couple of weeks. With your interest in history, you
shouldn't have much difficulty in genning up on
Revedon. Mrs Baxter would give you any help you
needed. What she doesn't know about the place isn't
worth knowing.'

Lian had come to a halt with her hand on their own bedroom doorknob. She wasn't sure what to think of the offer—although it certainly interested her.

'Are you serious?' she asked diffidently.

'I'd hardly be making the suggestion if I weren't,' he came back on a dry note. 'It would keep you occupied a couple of days a week, at least. Weekends, I'd bring in someone from town. That way, everyone would be happy.' He put his hand over hers to finish turning the knob, pushing open the door and forcing her to move ahead of him. 'We're going to be late for dinner if we don't get a move on.'

Lian waited until he closed the door again before turning resolutely to face him. 'Why?' she asked. 'You were dead set against it before.'

'Doubtful of the opportunities available,' he corrected. 'This idea only occurred this morning. It seemed to fit the bill.' The grey eyes were enigmatic. 'Was I wrong?'

She shook her head. 'No, I'd love to do it. I can't think of anything I'd like more, as a matter of fact.'

'Then that's settled.'

He was moving to pass her as he spoke. Lian made an instinctive move to block him. 'Bryn, I want you to believe there was no prior arrangement to meet Duncan this lunchtime. I don't even like the man very much.'

There was little change of expression in the lean features. 'All right,' he said, 'I believe it.'

She stared at him nonplussed. 'Just like that?'

His shrug was brief. 'One of us has to show a little faith. Are *you* going to believe I wasn't with Christine either?'

'Then who?' she asked, and saw his lips twist.

'Obviously not. Too bad.'

Lian resisted the impulse to reach out to him as he continued on his way across the spacious room. The doubts were still there; it was impossible to pretend otherwise. She only wished she could believe.

Fiona was already down when they reached the sitting-room at ten minutes to eight. She looked bone-weary, Lian thought.

'Busy afternoon,' she confirmed when asked. 'Lucky the lot Chris was after came up early. She was back in the shop by three.'

'Did she get the barometer?' queried Bryn on a casual note, without so much as a glance in Lian's direction.

'No,' regretfully. 'It went way above the limit, even for a Crichton. In fact, I'd say there isn't going to be much of a profit in it for the buyer.'

'Perhaps they wanted it for themselves,' Lian suggested, too well aware that along with that failure to secure went any tangible evidence that Bryn was telling the truth; Christine could easily have lingered long enough on her way back to the shop to lend weight to her story. 'I don't suppose everyone who attends an auction is a dealer.'

'You may be right,' her sister-in-law agreed. 'I tend to think of everything in terms of profit or loss these days.' She changed her tone to add, 'I gather you bought the pony?'

Bryn nodded. 'Nice little animal. But then, Paul would hardly have recommended it if it hadn't been. If the grey turns out as well as he sounds, we're in business there too. Are you seeing him tonight?'

Fiona's face seemed to close up. 'No,' she said shortly.

He made no attempt to pursue the subject, although his silence itself spoke volumes. To him there was no problem, Lian thought. If Fiona wanted Paul she had to be content to share him with his horses. Better that than another woman.

The evening was sultry, with the occasional roll of thunder in the distance. It would probably reach them around two in the morning, said Bryn over coffee on the terrace.

Clad in off-white trousers and black silk shirt open at the throat, he looked, to Lian's eyes at least, devastatingly masculine. She wanted desperately to be close to him, to have his lips on hers, his hands on her body. She could even, she felt, lay Christine's ghost given half a chance. Only she doubted if he would be making any move towards her tonight. Not after her refusal to grant him the benefit of the doubt earlier.

Looking up suddenly, he caught her eyes on him, the mocking lift of an eyebrow acknowledging the flush which tinged her cheeks. It was very likely that he knew exactly what she was thinking; a man like Bryn would always know when a woman was reacting to him. As she was his wife, there was nothing to stop her from taking the initiative herself, but she knew she wouldn't. That kind of gesture called for more self-assurance than she possessed. Supposing he turned away from her?

'I'll be going down to London again on Wednesday morning, by the way,' he announced. 'All being well, I'll be through by Friday.'

'And will that be it?' asked his mother.

'Should be. I'll be moving into the estate office as from Monday next.' He paused briefly, added without change of inflexion, 'Fleming will be moving on.'

'Really?' Mrs Thornley sounded surprised. 'I'd have thought he might like to take a little more time to find an alternative position. After all, he'd still be drawing an excellent salary.'

Bryn's shrug was non-committal. 'Money isn't everything.'

Try managing without it, reflected Lian drily. The news went some way towards explaining Duncan's attitude earlier, though. Whether Bryn had actually pressured him into leaving or it had been the man's own decision remained open to speculation. Ten to one he wouldn't be going without a substantial financial settlement, whichever, but that didn't mean he had to like it.

'I'm going up,' said Fiona, who had hardly spoken all evening. 'I feel like an early night.'

Lian stirred herself as the other rose to her feet. 'I think I'll do the same. This humidity is a bit too much.'

'It will cool down with the rain when it comes,' said Mrs Thornley comfortably. 'Stay and talk to me for a while, Bryn. We don't seem to have very much opportunity these days.'

'Of course.' The eyes meeting Lian's were devoid of promise. 'I'm not ready for bed yet either.'

CHAPTER TEN

GOING indoors with Fiona, Lian said lightly, 'I suppose all mothers lose out a little when their sons marry. More so, perhaps, than with daughters.'

'Considering she's still living in the same house as Bryn, that hardly applies to Mother,' the other returned. 'She's lucky to have a daughter-in-law who accepts it. I'm not sure I could.'

'It was her home long before it became mine—or Bryn's either, for that matter. How could I possibly resent it?' Lian hesitated before adding, 'Tell me to mind my own business if you want to, but is Bryn right about you and Paul?'

The answer came levelly enough. 'Up to a point. Horses aren't exactly my overriding passion, but I could take the stud if he'd only give on the show-jumping. He's the first to admit he's not top rank, but he still spends a good half of the year travelling round the country. Short of going with him, which would mean giving up *my* business interests, I'd hardly see anything of him from May right through October. Not a good basis for a marriage, would you say?'

'Not really,' Lian agreed. 'Does he know how you feel about it?'

'He'd have to be dense not to know, and he's far from that. So we either carry on the way we are, or we pack it in altogether.'

They had reached the top of the stairs. Lian paused, darting a sideways glance. 'Could you do that?'

'Not see him again?' Slim shoulders lifted. 'Might be best all round. I'm twenty-seven. Seeing you and Bryn and Jonathan together has made me realise what I'm missing. I'd like at least one child while I'm still the right side of thirty—preferably with a husband to boot.' She made a small wry gesture. 'That wasn't meant to be a dig at you.'

'It wasn't taken that way,' Lian assured her. 'Only, if it's Paul you love...'

'Not to say I couldn't fall for someone else.' The smile was reminiscent of her brother at his most cynical. 'There are more fish in the sea than ever came out of it. Anyway, I shouldn't be burdening you with my problems. Goodnight, Lian.'

She had obviously needed to talk to someone, Lian reflected as they parted company. Not that her contribution had been of much help. As to considering her own marriage a pattern to be emulated, that was a laugh in itself. She and Bryn were even further apart than Fiona and Paul, with as little chance of ever reaching a true understanding.

It was gone eleven when he eventually came up. In bed, but far from sleep, Lian made no attempt to pretend otherwise. Bryn had extended himself earlier; it was up to her now to make the same effort.

'Can we forget about Christine?' she asked as he began unfastening his shirt buttons.

'Do I take that to mean you believe I wasn't with her today?' came the smooth response.

Fingers crossed beneath the bed covers, she said, 'Yes.'

He eyed her consideringly for a moment, taking in the bareness of her shoulders above the sheet she had drawn across her breasts. 'Why the change of mind? As you so rightly concluded before dinner, there was no proof she attended the auction.'

'I don't have any proof that she didn't either,' Lian admitted. 'Only guesswork based on purely circumstantial evidence. If you say you were lunching with someone else, I believe you.'

'But you want me to say it again.' His tone was dry. 'All right, I was lunching with someone else. Only don't ask who, because I'm not prepared to go into it. Not right now, anyway.'

'I don't want to know,' she lied. 'I just want ... wanted ...'

The shrewd eyes were still on her face. 'Wanted what?' he prompted as her voice faltered.

'You.' It took all she had to force the word out.

His smile had an edge. 'And what makes you think you weren't going to get me regardless? I'm not into self-denial, as you may have noticed. Still, it's nice to know I'm not on my own when it comes to sexual proclivities after all.'

'Don't.' Her voice sounded husky. 'I didn't mean to say what I said last night, Bryn. It was just one thing leading to another.'

For a brief moment she thought her plea had fallen on deaf ears, then his face took on a wry cast. 'Not just on your side. I said a whole lot too much myself.'

He came to sit on the bed, bending his head to find her mouth in a kiss that stirred her soul with its unaccustomed tenderness. 'We have to work at it,' he murmured against her lips. 'More so than most.'

His shirt was open to the waist. Lian slid both her hands inside, fingertips tingling to the wiry feel of his body hair, the underlying hardness of muscle. She was nude beneath the single covering sheet. Bryn drew it away from her by slow degrees, following the material down to kiss each freshly exposed portion of pliant, quivering flesh with lips so firm and yet so sensitive. His hands were possessive, seeking and finding her most intimate self—rousing her to fever pitch in their mastery. She stifled the moans dragged from deep down in her throat against his shoulder, wanting him to stop, willing him to continue, wholly unable to contain the shuddering climax.

There was no holding back for either of them from there. Shorn of his clothing, he was all silk-clad muscle and rampant power, yet controllable too with the right approach. Lian learned fast and she learned well. If this was her one way of holding him then she would make it her life's work to be innovative, she vowed in the satiated aftermath. He was worth it because she loved him, and because one day he was going to love her the same way, no matter how long it took!

Tuesday was a brilliant day all round. Bryn waited until the Shetland had been delivered and settled down in his box for a few hours to recover from the upset of the journey before setting out to view his own proposed mount. Lian went with him because she couldn't bear to be parted. Jonathan elected to stay under the watchful eye of Ray and get to know his new friend, Rory.

The grey turned out to be a magnificent beast of seventeen hands. With enough spirit to stock a bar, Lian privately thought, watching the animal elude the man sent into the large fenced pen to attach a halter to the head collar already on. She had to bite down hard on her instinctive protest when Bryn elected to do the catching himself. If he was going to buy the animal, then he obviously had to be capable of mastering it.

Ears flicking, eyes suspicious, Silver stood still as Bryn approached. The latter was talking softly to the horse, although Lian couldn't hear what he was saying. Whatever it was, it appeared to be working. Apart from a toss of the beautiful head and a slight side-stepping movement, there was no objection to the halter being clipped on to the ring.

It was Bryn who did the saddling up too in the end. The animal's present owner—a man in his forties—seemed disinclined to go near. Silver laid his ears back and swung a wicked set of teeth when Bryn started to mount, but a sharp command to behave pulled him up with a jerk and a suddenly quizzical look, as if in fresh appraisal of this newcomer.

Seated, with the reins firmly secured, Bryn urged a walk and then a trot around the pen, and finally a slow canter. Man and horse looked magnificent together, Lian thought: both of them perfect specimens of the male gender. Silver would never be an easy ride—even she could tell that—but he was the right kind of animal for a man like Bryn.

Driving away from the place with the deal agreed, she said decisively, 'I'll go and see Paul about those lessons while you're looking round for a mare for me. That way, I should at least be capable of getting up on my own when the time comes.'

Bryn laughed. 'You'll make a fine horsewoman. You have the hands for it.' The last with a teasing, sideways glance. 'I should know!'

The longing to tell him how she felt about him was almost overwhelming. It took an effort to hold the words back. Too soon, she told herself. Give it a little more time. Perhaps if she got pregnant again...

'Is it absolutely essential for you to go to London tomorrow?' she asked.

'Afraid so.' He sounded regretful himself. 'I'll make sure I'm back on Friday, though.'

Silver would be there waiting for him, Lian reminded herself before reading too much into the strength of that avowal. She could begin to appreciate a little of what Fiona felt now. To the average woman, love was everything, while to a man it was only a part of his life. Not that she wouldn't be happy enough to settle for even that much, given the opportunity.

They spent an hour or so in the afternoon supervising Jonathan on his first foray into the joys of riding. Both child and pony were equally reluctant to be parted. It was only on reminder of Sam's prior claim that the leave-taking was finally accomplished.

Lian was grateful that Bryn hadn't attempted to lay down the law too strictly. The first flush of enthusiasm would soon settle down to a steadier pace. In the meantime, Samson was going to prove worth his weight in the persuasion stakes.

With half of August still to go, and the weather apparently recovered from last night's threatened recess, the days ahead held a whole lot of promise. Learning enough of Revedon's history to make her tours as interesting as Dorothy Baxter's was going to be a priority. And with Bryn right here on the estate, what more could she ask for the moment? It didn't do to be too greedy.

She found it hard, all the same, to reconcile herself to his departure the next morning, even if it was for a mere three days. With the forthcoming job in mind, she tagged on to Dorothy's two o'clock tour in order to study the presentation.

So different from the last time, when her mind had been on other matters, she thought, taking mental notes as she listened to the confident voice relating the story behind a certain ancestral portrait. Who could have imagined that the day would finish up the way it had? These were Jonathan's ancestors, the house and grounds themselves just a part of his inheritance. From rags to riches overnight didn't quite fit because they had never been quite that poor, but it was close enough.

Paul was delighted to hear she wanted lessons. He would be away himself as from the Friday, he said, but his manager could see to her needs just as well.

'Once you have a mount of your own, Bryn will be able to take you out himself, of course,' he added on Thursday morning, giving Lian a leg up on to the mare he had spoken of. 'Lady here would be ideal for you. We'll stick to the near pasture today until you find your balance. You've a good natural seat, so it shouldn't take long.'

It didn't. Within half an hour, Lian had mastered both the trot and the slow canter, and was wondering how she could ever have hesitated over taking up the pastime. To be up there in the saddle with the warm animal smell in her nostrils and the feel of silken muscles moving to her command was sheer exhilaration.

'Thought of doing any jumping?' asked Paul when they took a break at his suggestion before she got saddle sore.

Lian laughed. 'One thing at a time! Right now, I'll settle quite happily for this.' She waited a moment before seizing on the opening, too well aware of treading a fine line between friendly concern and downright interference. 'Don't you ever get fed up of travelling round so much every summer?'

'As a matter of fact,' he said on a rueful note, 'I'm thinking of making this one the last. There was a time when I could at least put up a fair performance, but lately I seem to have lost the incentive. Horses sense a lack of commitment. They won't bother trying if you don't.'

She said softly, 'Does Fiona know?'

Brown eyes acquired a sudden closed look, like a shutter coming down. 'I doubt if she'd be interested.'

'I think she might.' Lian tried to keep her tone casual. 'Can we go round again?'

'Sure.' Paul's voice revealed nothing. 'We'll take a ride up alongside the copse and back.'

Arriving home in time to change from the jodhpurs and shirt she had bought the previous day into something more suited to the luncheon table, Lian felt a warm glow of accomplishment. Bryn would buy the mare if she asked, and they could ride together every day. The more they shared, the closer they would become.

With regard to Fiona's problem, she wasn't at all sure what would happen. Paul had only said he was thinking of giving up show-jumping. When it came to the actual doing, it may be another matter. She couldn't even mention it to Fiona herself because the other would suspect her of disclosing a confidence. It had to be up to the two of them to sort themselves out.

Mrs Thornley listened to her glowing account of the morning's activities with indulgence. It had been several years since she had last ridden herself, she said, but she could appreciate the feeling.

'I think it's time you started calling me Mother,' she declared with an air of decision, halfway through the meal. 'You've fitted in very well here, Lian. Better, I have to admit, than I anticipated.'

'Me too?' asked Jonathan, and received a fond smile.

'Of course, darling. You're a very good boy, most of the time.'

'I'm a good boy *all* of the time!' came the indignant reply, causing both women to stifle smiles. 'Me and Sam and Rory are all good boys.' He added without pause, 'When is Daddy coming home?'

'Tomorrow,' Lian assured him for the umpteenth time, and felt a warm inner glow at the thought. She couldn't wait to see him again herself.

It took Fiona's arrival an hour or so later with Christine in tow to put a blight on the day.

'Early closing,' the former explained. 'We're going to the pool until teatime. Why don't you join us?'

About to make some excuse, Lian caught Christine's eye and realised the other was expecting just that. 'Good idea,' she said instead. 'I left a suit over there this morning when Jonathan and I were in.'

'Where is he now?' queried Christine. Her smile was all surface, voice cool. 'I'd have thought you wouldn't dare let a four-year-old out of your sight with so many total strangers about the place.'

'He's having his afternoon rest,' Lian replied, equally coolly. 'In any case, he can't get out of the private gardens.'

'I'll bring him over to you when he comes down,' offered Mrs Thornley. 'He's had a busy morning, so he'll probably sleep till around three.'

Going over to the pool, Lian listened to the other two discussing some minor point of business and tried to overcome her antipathy towards the woman Bryn had been involved with at one time, if not recently. It was Christine herself who made it so difficult. Her whole attitude was one of utter animosity. As Fiona's partner, she was obviously going to be in the picture to a certain extent. That fact had to be faced. No matter what he might have felt—or even still feel—for the woman, Bryn had to be relied upon not to do anything about it.

Stripped to a bright pink bikini of only minimal coverage, the other's well-endowed figure made Lian feel like an underdeveloped teenager. Rather *too* voluptuous for so brief a bikini, she comforted herself, although she doubted if the average man would see it quite the same way.

The three of them swam and splashed around for a while, then relaxed on loungers to dry off in the sunshine. Restless, Fiona was up again within minutes and making a seemingly earnest attempt at the backstroke speed record.

'The sooner she gives Paul the push, the better,' remarked Christine without lifting her head from its supine position. 'No man is worth that much!'

'*No* man?' asked Lian softly, and gained a reaction in the sudden compression of bright pink lips.

'The only reason you're married to Bryn is sleeping upstairs right now,' she returned hardily. 'He wasn't going to turn his back on his own son, as you very well knew. You don't mean anything to him, and you never will. You don't have what it takes to fit in.'

She had laid herself wide open to that, Lian thought painfully. Not that she was about to reveal how deep the barb had gone. 'And you do, I suppose?' she said with control.

'Of course. My family have been landowners in Cumbria for generations. Not on as grand a scale as Revedon, perhaps, but the breeding is there. What background can you claim?'

'My paternal grandfather was a solicitor, like my father after him,' Lian replied. 'Before that, I've never bothered to find out.'

'Perhaps as well.' The sneer was calculated. 'Lucky for you Bryn is liberal-minded. Otherwise, you might have found yourself minus a husband *and* a son.'

That wasn't even worth answering, Lian decided. All the same, the exchange had hit hard enough to undermine what confidence she had managed to accumulate. Christine was the kind of wife Bryn had needed, not some nonentity from the sticks.

Her self-esteem was back up several points again by morning. Allowing someone like Christine to get to her that way was ridiculous, Lian told herself firmly. She knew Bryn didn't love her, but that was no reason to suppose he entertained the same notions Christine harboured regarding family background. Mrs Thornley herself had expressed satisfaction, and she was no easy conquest.

She had herself well enough in hand to go out with Jonathan to greet Bryn when he arrived home in mid-afternoon.

'All settled but the dust,' he confirmed in answer to her question. He hadn't offered to kiss her, nor she him. The grey eyes scanning her face held a curious expression. 'You look tired. Been overdoing it?'

'Never tell a woman she looks tired,' Lian responded lightly. 'It's like saying she looks old!'

His laugh was dry. 'At twenty-four, that's hardly likely.' With Jonathan skipping on ahead, they moved towards the house. At the door, he reiterated, 'So what *have* you been doing with yourself?'

'Learning to ride, for one thing,' Lian acknowledged. 'Paul thinks I have a good seat.'

'Paul's not wrong,' came the droll retort, 'but what about the riding?'

Her own laugh had a sparkle to it. 'Coming along nicely. The mare I'm using is on offer, by the way, if you're interested.'

'If you like her, we'll take her,' he said. 'Did Silver get here yet?'

'This morning as promised. Ray has him settled in nicely, although he kicked up a bit when they got him out of the trailer.'

'Probably doesn't like travelling.' Bryn didn't sound too concerned. 'I'll go over after tea and take a look.'

She would only go with him if invited, thought Lian. Some things he might prefer to do alone. In the meantime, she could enjoy just having him home again.

Jonathan accompanied him upstairs when he went to change from the suit in which he had travelled, chattering nineteen to the dozen the whole way. Lian could hear Bryn's deeper tones getting in the occasional comment, then they were round the curve and out of both sight and hearing. She had to thank her lucky stars that Bryn had adapted to fatherhood so swiftly and so well, she acknowledged, going to join Mrs Thornley in the sitting-room. It might have been so different. But then, how many other men would have been as quick to put the matter on an official footing in the first place? He was one in a million. Whatever happened, he would always be that.

She tried not to mind too much when he went off to the stables on his own after tea. He needed no distractions while getting reacquainted with the stallion. Fiona telephoned around six o'clock to say she would be eating at Long Acres. Her mood was difficult to judge over the line, but Lian kept her fingers crossed for a happy outcome. If Fiona and Paul could make a go of their relationship, it would somehow hold out hope for her and Bryn.

He came back in time to say goodnight to Jonathan. After dinner he suggested a walk in the grounds, to which Lian readily agreed. Strolling together round the lake in the scented darkness, they seemed easier together than they had ever been. All she needed right now, Lian thought wistfully, was his arm about her shoulders to make things near perfect.

'It's good to be home,' he said on a note of content. 'I lost the urge to be out there in the thick of it. From now on it's Revedon all the way. We have to preserve it for Jonathan, and for his children after him.'

'That's looking a long way ahead,' Lian said lightly. 'I can't imagine you as a grandfather—all silver hair and shaky limbs!'

'And you with your hair in a bun and spectacles on the end of your nose,' he mocked back. He laughed, shaking his head. 'You're right, it is looking too far ahead. Here and now is enough to be going on with.'

More than enough for her, Lian reflected. Aloud she said, 'Shall you be keeping office hours when you get started?'

It took him a moment to reply. When he did speak, his tone was neutral. 'Initially there'll be a lot of sorting out to do. I've suspected for some time that Fleming was working to his own advantage, but I didn't realise the half of it until I began taking a serious interest.'

Lian looked up with suddenly widened eyes. 'You mean he's been defrauding the estate?'

'With a vengeance. He suspects I know it too, which is why I arranged to meet my solicitor at the White Hart to discuss proceedings instead of going to the office. What I didn't anticipate was being followed out there.'

Lian had stopped walking. She said slowly, 'If he was following you, he was hardly going to arrange a meeting with me at the same time and place.'

'That did occur to me eventually. Seeing you in the car with him was enough to cancel out straight thinking for some time. My one idea was to get back here and confront you with it.'

She searched his face, trying to read the mind behind the enigmatic grey eyes. 'I wasn't thinking very straight myself,' she admitted. 'I was so sure you and Christine...' She let the words fade away on seeing the fleeting spark they struck, and said instead, 'So what happens now? Is he going to be arrested?'

'First thing Monday morning—if he's still here by then.'

'You mean you've giving him the chance to get away scot-free?'

Bryn shrugged. 'Could be less trouble in the long run than dragging it out through the courts. He's been clever. It's going to take a very fine-tooth comb to get at the full story—if we ever do. Without a reference, he doesn't stand a chance of getting another similar position, which will be some retribution. It's up to him. He can either vanish over the weekend, or take his chances with the law.'

'You've actually told him that?'

'Not in so many words. I doubt if I needed to.' Bryn made a sudden incisive movement. 'Anyway, that's it. Let's get back to the house.'

Telling her at all had served little real purpose, Lian conceded as they retraced their steps, but she was glad that he had seen fit to confide in her. It wasn't until much later, lying in his arms with the thunder of her heartbeats still ringing in her ears, that she thought how much better it would be if Christine would only vanish over the weekend too.

Fiona was at breakfast, and looking considerably happier than she had of late. She didn't mention Paul, but Lian was almost sure he was the root cause of the change in her.

The announcement that Christine was selling out her share in the business came as a complete and total shock. Judging from Bryn's reaction, he hadn't known about it either, Lian judged. Not that he was giving much away even now.

'A rather sudden decision, isn't it?' commented Mrs Thornley.

'It's been on the cards for quite a while,' Fiona admitted. 'I considered buying her out myself, but I didn't fancy the idea of running the whole show on my own. Anyway, Liz Davenport is coming in with me. She's always taken a keen interest, and we get along so well. Chris's brother and his wife have a string of beauty salons in the south. She'll be joining them as from the end of next week.'

'Seems to have worked out well all round,' said Bryn on a casual note that gave no clue to his inner emotions. 'Why don't you ask the Davenports over? I haven't seen Roger in months.'

'Will do.' Fiona swallowed the last dregs of her coffee and got to her feet. 'Must be off. I'll be out to dinner again, by the way.'

There was a small silence after she had departed. Jonathan was the first to break it. 'Are you coming to the stables, Daddy?'

'I'll follow you in a few minutes,' came the response. 'I have a couple of things to take care of first.'

Like phoning Christine? Lian wondered, taking care not to look at him directly. Another week, and the woman would be gone altogether. She could surely allow him that much.

With less than an hour to go before the first visitors would arrive, she thought it inadvisable to take Samson with them to the stables in case they ran into any children. His size tended to frighten most. Jonathan found this difficult to understand. Despite his own comparative lack of stature, he had never known a moment's hesitation where the dog was concerned—nor the Shetland either, for that matter. He had a way with animals that could only, Lian was sure, be inherited from his father.

There was no sign of Ray when they reached the yard. Not all that surprising, Lian conceded, as they hadn't let him know they were on their way. Rory was in the loose-box next to the tack-room. He came to Jonathan's call, pushing his head over the specially lowered half-door in greeting.

'Better wait till Ray comes,' said Lian when it was suggested that a saddle was fetched. 'Let's go and have a look at Silver while we're waiting.'

The stallion was moving restlessly in the larger box next door. Lian lifted Jonathan up to see him, making sure to keep him well clear of the doorway. It was all very well to be without fear, but there was nothing predictable about this particular animal.

Ears twitching forwards, he turned his head to look when Jonathan spoke to him, but made no move to approach. He really was a superb specimen, Lian thought admiringly. She could understand why Bryn had wanted him.

Not that anyone else would be riding him, Ray included. The latter didn't believe in taking unnecessary risks, he had said after narrowly escaping decapitation from a lashing pair of hoofs on getting the horse from trailer to loose-box the previous morning.

Seeing Duncan Fleming standing a few yards away as she dropped Jonathan back on his feet, she felt her heart give a nasty little lurch. Eyes narrowed, face hewn from solid granite, he looked disturbingly cold and calculating.

'You startled me!' she exclaimed in an effort to cover her involuntary reaction. 'I didn't realise anyone else was here.'

'I just arrived,' he said. 'Something I had to do before I went. Don't bother pretending you don't know what I'm talking about,' he added in the same passionless but no less threatening tones. 'You've got it made here, haven't you, girl?'

'Bryn will be along any minute,' she lied. 'I'd get going while the going is still good, if I were you. If he finds you here——'

'He won't.' He was moving as he spoke, the sheer menace of him causing her to fall back instinctively. 'I was going to leave a message with this beast of his, but I've got a better idea now.'

Understanding little of what was going on, but frightened by the very atmosphere, Jonathan clung to Lian as she put her arm protectively about him. The animal in the box right behind them was reacting to the tension in the air with agitation. Lian made an attempt to break away to the side, but was foiled by the swiftness of the man whose intention was becoming all too horribly clear. Seizing her roughly by the arm, he unlatched the half-door and thrust both her and the child still clinging to her inside the box, slamming both top and bottom sections with a force that set the highly strung horse rearing into the air.

In the moments following, Lian could only crouch by the wall and try to protect her son from the flailing hoofs as the maddened animal vented its spleen. It was a nightmare with sound effects, the whinnies deafening in the darkened confines. Even a glancing blow from one of those steel-tipped feet could be a killer. It seemed impossible that they hadn't yet connected.

Jonathan saved the day for them both. The clear childish treble carried with surprising strength: 'Don't be a silly billy, Silver! You're just showing off!'

The stallion came to a sudden quivering halt, blowing hard through his nostrils and obviously still on edge, but miraculously quietened. Jonathan wriggled free before Lian could stop him, and went right up to the animal

to stroke between the muscular forelegs, which was as
far up as he could reach.

'It was only a door banging,' he said comfortingly.
'There's nothing going to hurt you.'

Leaning weakly against the wall of the box, Lian felt
hysterical laughter welling in her throat. Like father, like
son: nothing daunted a true Thornley!

The top half of the door was opened again suddenly
from outside. Bryn's stunned expression when he saw
her standing there made her want to laugh again—or
cry. 'Come along now, Jonathan,' she said, and thought
how odd her voice sounded. 'Daddy will see to him.'

Bryn let them both out of the box, closing the door
again on the now quite docile animal. 'What the devil
possessed you to go in there?' he demanded harshly. 'I
heard the racket he was kicking up from way off! You
might both had been killed——!' He broke off, the anger
in his eyes giving way to some other emotion less easily
defined as he registered Lian's uncontrollable trembling
and paper-white face. Next moment she was in his arms
and he was holding her tight, voice muffled and rough
against her hair. 'You could have been killed!'

Jonathan had gone to look in on Rory. Grown-ups
made an awful lot of fuss about nothing, he told the
pony. Silver had just been throwing a tantrum, that was
all. If he'd wanted to kick them he would have done.
Anybody knew that.

Lian knew only one thing. She wanted Bryn to go on
holding her like this. It wasn't so much what he had said
but the way he had said it that was important. He had
to care, to have infused that amount of feeling into his
voice.

'The top door was latched,' he said suddenly on a totally different note. 'It couldn't have blown to accidentally!' He held her away from him, searching her face. 'What happened?'

'Duncan Fleming,' she got out. 'He wanted to leave you a memento. I think he intended doing something to Silver initially.'

'Nothing to what I'll do to him when I lay hands on him!' There was a killing fury in the grey eyes. 'He can't have got very far.'

Lian clutched at his sleeve as he started to turn. 'He isn't worth it, Bryn! Let the police take care of him. *Please.*'

For a brief moment he seemed on the verge of ignoring her plea, then he let out his breath on a harsh sigh. 'I've no idea which way he'll be heading, anyway, so it would be pretty futile. We'll go on back to the house. I have his car registration on file. The police can put out an all points bulletin. Attempted murder is more than enough to be going on with.'

Jonathan expressed reluctance to leave without the ride he had been looking forward to, but a word from his father was all it took to settle the matter. There was still no sign of Ray. Lian hoped there would be no repercussions for the man, although she feared the worst. Bryn would be almost certain to lay some blame for the incident at his door. If he had been here at his post, Duncan would have been forced to abandon his plans.

Events moved swiftly from there. The police arrived within twenty minutes, statements were taken, and procedures set into motion. Lian could sense Bryn's impatience with the whole process, but it had to be gone through. All they could do now was sit back and wait for the man to be picked up.

'You should go and lie down for a while, Lian,' suggested Mrs Thornley concernedly after the police had departed. 'You look very pale still.'

'Just a bit of a headache,' she admitted. 'Reaction, I suppose. Perhaps I will.'

'I'll bring you some aspirin,' offered Bryn.

She was lying on the bed when he came up. He fetched a glass of water from the bathroom for her, sitting down on the edge of the bed to extend a palm holding the two white tablets, and watch her swallow them.

'If I'd lost you, life wouldn't have been worth living,' he said on a rough note. 'Do you have any idea how much I love you, Lian?'

'No,' she murmured huskily.

His lips twisted. 'Hardly surprising. I didn't fully appreciate it myself up until an hour or so ago. I think it must have begun the very first time I saw you at that party. You made every other girl there look insipid. I wanted you badly enough to disregard any warning signs—and there must have been some.'

Lian put up a hand and rested it against the lean brown cheek, her eyes misty. 'I wanted you to make love to me that night, Bryn. It wasn't just the champagne. I suppose deep down I wanted the first time to be wonderful, and with you I knew it would be. And it was. Nothing can ever change that.'

Taking the hand, he pressed it to his lips. 'Finding out how old you really were knocked me for six,' he admitted wryly. 'My first inclination was to get out fast. Letting you go home alone in that taxi was a shameful thing to do, even if it did take me a while to acknowledge it. I could have found you if I'd put my mind to it. If the truth were known, I was relieved at the time to have the excuse.'

'It wouldn't have been any good even if you had managed to find me again,' she said. 'I hated you for a while—nearly as much as I hated myself. Until I actually held him, I sometimes hated the baby as well.'

'That's not surprising either. That one night changed your whole life.' He smoothed the tumbled hair back from her face in a gesture so tender it made her heart ache. 'I can't do anything about those years you had to live through on your own, but I can at least try to make the future worthwhile.'

Green eyes glowed with an inner light. 'You already did. Why do you think I've been so jealous of Christine? I couldn't bear to think of you with her.'

'There was never very much between us at all,' he said. 'It was finished before you came along, in any case, although I have to admit I had some difficulty getting it across to her. At best, she couldn't hold a candle to you, my darling. When you walked back into my life four weeks ago I was given a whole new lease.' His smile was reminiscent. 'In more ways than one.' The smile disappeared again. 'Then this business with Fleming cropped up. Not that I imagined he'd go to these kinds of lengths.'

Lian shook her head. 'Let's forget about him for now. There are more important things to think about.'

He looked back at her without concealment, mouth slowly widening. 'What about your headache?' he asked.

'Gone for good,' she said, and found a moment to be sorry for all the women in the world who weren't loved by a man like Bryn.

HARLEQUIN PROUDLY PRESENTS A DAZZLING CONCEPT IN ROMANCE FICTION

 One small town,
twelve terrific love stories

JOIN US FOR A YEAR IN THE FUTURE OF TYLER

Each book set in Tyler is a self-contained love story; together,
the twelve novels stitch the fabric of the community.

LOSE YOUR HEART TO TYLER!

Join us for the second TYLER book, BRIGHT HOPES, by
Pat Warren, available in April.

*Former Olympic track star Pam Casals arrives in Tyler to
coach the high school team. Phys ed instructor Patrick
Kelsey is first resentful, then delighted. And rumors fly about
the dead body discovered at the lodge.*

Following the success of WITH THIS RING, Harlequin cordially invites you to enjoy the romance of the wedding season with

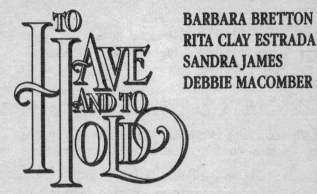

BARBARA BRETTON
RITA CLAY ESTRADA
SANDRA JAMES
DEBBIE MACOMBER

A collection of romantic stories that celebrate the joy, excitement, and mishaps of planning that special day by these four award-winning Harlequin authors.

Available in April at your favorite Harlequin retail outlets.

ZODIAC WORD SEARCH CONTEST

You can win a year's supply of Harlequin romances ABSOLUTELY FREE! All you have to do is complete the word puzzle below and send it to us so we receive it by April 30, 1992. The first 10 properly completed entries chosen by random draw will win a year's supply of Harlequin romances (four books every month, one from each of four of the series Harlequin publishes—worth over $150.00). What could be easier?

NEXT MONTH: LOOK FOR YOUR CHANCE TO WIN AN OLD-TIME RADIO!!!!!

S	E	C	S	I	P	R	I	A	M	F
I	U	L	C	A	N	C	E	R	L	I
S	A	I	N	I	M	E	G	N	S	R
C	A	P	R	I	C	O	R	N	U	E
S	E	I	R	A	N	G	I	S	I	O
Z	O	D	W	A	T	E	R	B	R	I
O	G	A	H	M	A	T	O	O	A	P
D	R	R	T	O	U	N	I	R	U	R
I	I	B	R	O	R	O	M	G	Q	O
A	V	I	A	N	U	A	N	C	A	C
C	E	L	E	O	S	T	A	R	S	S

Used with permission of D. J. Verrells.

PISCES   ARIES
CANCER   GEMINI
SCORPIO   TAURUS
AQUARIUS   LIBRA
CAPRICORN   SAGITTARIUS
LEO   EARTH
VIRGO   STAR
FIRE   SIGN
WATER   MOON
ZODIAC   AIR

HOW TO ENTER

All the words listed are hidden in the word puzzle grid. You can find them by reading the letters forward, backward, up and down, or diagonally. When you find a word, circle it or put a line through it. Don't forget to fill in your name and address in the space provided, put this page in an envelope, and mail it today to:

Harlequin Word Puzzle Contest
Harlequin Reader Service®
P.O. Box 9071
Buffalo, NY 14269-9071

NAME _____

ADDRESS _____

_____

CITY _____ STATE _____ ZIP CODE _____

Janet Dailey ®
Americana

Janet Dailey's perennially popular Americana series
continues with more exciting states!

Don't miss this romantic tour of America through
fifty favorite Harlequin Presents novels, each one set
in a different state, and researched by Janet and her
husband, Bill.

A journey of a lifetime in one cherished collection.

April titles	#29 NEW HAMPSHIRE *Heart of Stone*
	#30 NEW JERSEY *One of the Boys*